Montreal Literary Society

The Essays of the Literary Society

Read in Montreal during the winter of 1880-81

Montreal Literary Society

The Essays of the Literary Society
Read in Montreal during the winter of 1880-81

ISBN/EAN: 9783337255558

Printed in Europe, USA, Canada, Australia, Japan

Cover: Foto ©Andreas Hilbeck / pixelio.de

More available books at **www.hansebooks.com**

THE ESSAYS

—OF THE—

LITERARY SOCIETY,

READ IN MONTREAL DURING THE WINTER OF
1880· 81, AT THE HOUSES OF SOME OF
ITS MEMBERS.

Nos hæc novimus esse nihil. ,MART.

1881.

PREFACE.

In Montreal, three years ago, at the suggestion of a few persons interested in English Literature, a small Society was formed which met once every week to discuss authors who are part of the literary store of all readers. Time has dealt kindly with the social endeavour, and it has been thought advisable to have a memento of the pleasant hours spent during the winter of 1880-81, by printing the series of Essays read to the Society by its members. It may be added, that in regard to matter, the subsequent pages stand as they were written; also, that it has been deemed right to preserve even their form, at the risk of irregularity of appearance. The Essays are arranged in order of subject, not of delivery, and although containing subjects for the critic's eye, are not published for the eye of the critic. If some motto were needed to indicate the Society's estimate of the worth of its work, except to itself, these words from Martial would suffice :

" Nos hæc novimus esse nihil."

The Society has long lacked the convenience of a name ; by most of its members it has, of late, been known by the title which appears on the cover, while to a very few of them that title may still be a novelty.

CONTENTS.

ADDISON'S ESSAYS ON BALLADS.

CHEVY CHACE AND THE BABES IN THE WOOD.

"Spectator." Nos. 70, 74, 85.

Addison's design in writing these Essays, was to cultivate a purer taste in literature, by calling the public attention to those ballads, *once* the delight of all men, but, owing to the artificial spirit of the age, *now* much overlooked or forgotten. They existed only in mutilated MSS., and printed scraps, scattered about over the country, or hidden away in libraries. It was a bold task, there-fore, to hold up to admiration that which was scorned and neglected by all ; but Addison, sure of his ground, did not shrink from encountering ridicule, and there is no doubt that such criticism from so competent a judge had even more effect than he anticipated.

Fifty-four years later, in 1765, Bishop Percy, after spending much time in collecting and revising these scattered fragments, published his Reliques, and in his notes made mention of Addison's criticism. His collection was favourably received, and besides inspiring many individuals, exerted a very healthful influence over poetry in general, by introducing a new, or rather old, but forgotten element. Others have followed his example, and copies have been so multiplied that in our day an Essay upon Ballads would need no apology. The following information is taken chiefly from Percy.

He tells us that "the minstrels were an order of men in the middle ages, who subsisted by the arts of poetry and music, and sang to the harp verses com-posed either by themselves or others." The Normans greatly encouraged this class in England, and they flourished for many centuries after the Conquest.

The minstrels are generally represented as coming from the "North Coun-tree," which accounts for the prevalence of the Northern dialect in their compo-sitions, as also for a certain romantic wildness, and for the fact that many of the subjects related to the Border feuds. Thus the long continued quarrels of the Percy and the Douglas gave rise to the Ballad of Chevy Chace.

As the minstrel art declined, many recited only the compositions of others, yet scrupled not to change whole verses or insert new ones at their own con-venience, and this explains the great variation in different MSS.

In the reign of Elizabeth the old order had died out ; indeed a representation of a bard was a curiosity provided for her entertainment at the great feast given by the Earl of Leicester. A new race of Ballad-makers then sprang up, who wrote narrative songs for the press. These were written in the Northern dia-lect and in exacter measure, with a correctness which sometimes bordered on insipidity, yet they were occasionally very simple and pathetic. To this class we may refer the Babes in the Wood.

CHEVY CHACE.—In regard to "Chevy Chace," Percy tells us that the Ballad, as criticised by Addison, was the only copy then known, but did not date back further than the reign of Queen Elizabeth. He gives also in his collection what he considers to be the genuine, antiqu) song (date, Henry VI.), referred to by Sir Philip Sidney. This fact would account for Addison's dissent from Sidney's opinion concerning " the rude style and evil apparel of the song," as expressed in Essay 74.

Bishop Percy thinks that probably the criticism of the Elizabethan poet led to a revisal of the Ballad, resulting in one written in more modern language, and improved in style and versification, though occasionally falling short of the original in force and dignity.

Although the story of Chevy Chace has no sanction in history, yet it is probably a comparatively true account of an incident in connection with the Border feuds between the families of Percy and Douglas, which became in some way entangled with the facts of the Battle of Otterbourne (1388), where the heads of both houses fell.

ANALYSIS OF ESSAY.—Addison introduces his subject by stating that what is *natural* appeals to the sympathies of human beings in whatever class of life they may be found, as human nature is the same everywhere ; and that what pleases a multitude, even of common people, must have in it an element which can be appreciated by all.

He then describes the effect of the natural and artificial styles of writing, placing the Ballad with the works of Homer, Virgil, and Milton in the former class, and quotes the opinions of three great men in regard to the ballad of Chevy Chace, in particular those which coincide with his own.

He justifies his classification by comparing this popular song with the ancient models, and shows that they agree in their obedience to the rules. Firstly, "That an heroic poem should be founded upon some important precept of morality adapted to the constitution of the country in which the poet writes," and secondly, that it should celebrate "persons and actions which do honour to their own country," while at the same time it justly acknowledges merit and bravery, by whomsoever shown.

In the beginning of Essay 74, Addison explains that the similarity in the natural, simple, and poetical sentiments, which exists between the classic models, and the Ballad in question, does not result from plagiarism, but from an inspiration of the same kind of poetical genius. He also gives it as his opinion that had the song been more embellished it might have pleased an artificial taste, but could not have moved to such a degree the heart of a Sidney. He then carries the comparison, begun in the former Essay, even more into detail, supporting his remarks by many quotations, and ending with an apology for so doing, saying that he thought it necessary to have his opinion in this matter confirmed by great authorities, as it was opposed by the popular taste.

The Children in the Wood, is also given by Bishop Percy, who thinks that the story is taken from an old play, entitled, "Two Lamentable Tragedies, the one of a chandler in Thames Street, the other of a young child murthered in a word by two ruffians, with the consent of his unkle," the scene of which is laid in Padua. This play, however, was published in 1601, and it has since been proved that the Ballad was entered in the Stationers' Books at an earlier date ; it appears also from internal evidence to be thoroughly English. The simple and natural way in which the story is told, would of itself lead us to suppose that it is the account of some actual occurrence which is here given.

Addison introduces his criticism by giving many examples of the not uncom-mon fate of literary fragments, namely, to serve the purpose of wrappers, lin-ings, etc., and states that his habit of examining such scraps, led to the discovery of the treasure on which his Essay is written.

He represents the beauty of The Children in the Wood, to consist in its being a true copy of nature, while the simplicity of its style, its genuine and unaffected sentiments and touching incidents, would always ensure its popular-ity, notwithstanding the want of ornament and the plainness of expression which characterize it.

He then instances three great men who were ballad-lovers, and the Essay is closed by a parting hit at the conceited wits of the day, whose want of apprecia-tion of a touch of nature in her naked simplicity, was not to be wondered at, as they were incapable of admiring her, even when adorned by art.

A. E. R.

ADDISON'S ESSAYS ON MILTON'S PARADISE LOST.

The Essays on Milton, which we have read to-night, form part of a series of Essays or disquisitions on semi-religious, literary and philosophical subjects which appeared in the *Spectator* every Saturday, and which were written by Addison, and were designed by him for reading on the following Sunday.

These Saturday papers are conspicuous for their literary and intellectual merit, and stand out prominently in this respect, among the lighter and more frivolous Essays of the *Spectator* written by Steele.

The popular and social side of society Steele could portray with consummate skill, but he had neither the learning, nor the taste, nor the critical acuteness to qualify him to cope with the more abstract and more elevated subjects which were designed to foster a taste for a higher tone of literature, and to elevate and refine public taste and morals. It was by thus treating of elevated subjects in an elevated yet simple manner, that Addison did so much to accomplish this end. On these Saturday papers Addison's reputation as an Essayist is chiefly founded ; a reputation which justly overshadows that of his less profound associate.

But to return to the subject of our reading for this evening, Milton's Paradise Lost. Addison in reviewing or criticising Paradise Lost in these Essays, does not follow the mode or process of criticism usually pursued at the present day, of judging and appreciating the poem or work by itself, or upon its own merits, but he proceeds entirely by way of comparison, and discovers beauties or defects in the Miltonic song, in so far as it exceeds, or falls short of, the Iliad or Æneid, and conserves or departs from the rigid classic rules by which these poems are modelled.

Such a mode of criticism, I submit, is not fairly applicable to such a man as Milton when singing such a song ; a man whose genius and whose subject relieved him from the observance of these "nicer laws" upon which technical critics insist.

The result of Addison's comparison and criticism establish, undoubtedly, that *even technically*, Milton was a greater poet than either Homer or Virgil, but I take exception to Addison's mode of critical procedure, on the ground that it is artistically a false mode of establishing the merits of any work. Who, for instance, would ever think of attempting to point out the beauties of the Scriptures by comparing them with Joseph Smith's Bible ? Absolute and not relative criticism is the test which should be applied to literary works of the highest order.

To one other point would I call the attention of the meeting, inasmuch as it may be of interest to several of the members.

In speaking of Milton's unequalled powers of IMAGINATION, or FANCY, Addison again advances the theory first expounded and enunciated by him in the Essay on the Pleasures of the Imagination, but now universally admitted, "That the Pleasures of the Imagination flow from visible objects only, and that the imagination can proceed from, or be exercised with regard to these objects only which are before our eyes or have been taken in through the vision ;" or to put it more briefly, *that we cannot imagine what is not.* The question opens a large field for discussion.

And lastly the criticisms on Addison's Essays on Milton have been numerous and not always favourable. They have been adjudged to be "not very profound," "to be wanting in logical sequence," "to be austentatiously pedantic," but be this as it may : in the opinion of every scholar, of every Christian, and of every Englishman, they are entitled to a high place in the literature of Britain inasmuch as in them we find the first public recognition of the grandeur and beauty of Milton's chiefest work, and of the merit of England's greatest poet.

C. J. F.

RICHARD STEELE.

As one of the papers chosen for the night's reading is from the hand of Steele, we have come upon a new character, having for itself an interest greater than that inspired by the calmer and colder Addison.

What we know of the story of Richard Steele's life is of uncommon value to those who enjoy the contemplation of unaffected humanity. His father was secretary to the Duke of Ormond in Dublin, where the Essayist first saw the light in 1671. He inherited from an Irish mother all the most generous quali-ties which mark the people of her land. All but those of strong national bias must have suspended the usual admiring phrase at first sight of him, for if we are in any way to trust the cruel pen of Dennis, the infant was not beautiful. A very unflattering description of the outside of the man, which Thackeray says is dreadfully exact, was given by his contemporary ; it was softened only by the statement that he had been born with his native country stamped upon his face. The boy lost his father when he was in his fifth year, and he was left alone with his mother, whom he remembered with much tenderness all his life. Not long after she died, too, and young Steele was freed from the strongest though softest restraint his nature could have had.

The kind Duke sent him to the Charterhouse School, where his time was no doubt carelessly spent, like his after-life at College. To the study of books he applied himself little, but his eyes were always open with good-natured curiosity to the living world around him. The friendship, to which both Addison and Steele owed much of their individual fame, was formed at the Charterhouse, the latter having the praise of being the more ardent in the attachment. At Ox-ford, Steele first tried his pen at comedy, but did not distinguish himself there in that or anything more solid. Before his term was well out, he jumped from the academic gown into the gorgeous shell of a horse-guardsman. When Addi-son came back from the Continent in 1702, he found him a Captain in Lucas's Fusiliers, and given up to the most extravagant jollity. He had in the previ-ous year written a religious treatise called The Christian Hero, trusting that such work would wean him from the convivial bowl, but the course of composi-tion had been intermitted by spells of deplorable tipsiness, and the treatment failed. The nearness of his old adored schoolmaster must have placed somewhat of a check on his rioting, and we find him producing a clever farcical comedy in 1703, which has some of Addison's strokes. When the fortunes of his friend took a sudden turn, Steele left the army and followed in the road to honour. After bringing him a pretty fortune, his first wife had died, and anon the widower ardently wooes and wins the lovely Mrs. Scurlock. His dear Prue pre-served all the letters to himself—about four hundred—that she had from him as lover and husband, and they are the most important record we have of his many odd doings. In a letter to her mother on the 3rd September, 1707, he pu's his income at £1,025 per annum, and, says he, "I promise myself the pleasure of an industrious and virtuous life in studying to do things agreeable to you." Four days after Dick married the daughter. His mother-in-law had a life interest in the estate, and kept him from going too far with that. Among many little similar notes, there was one sent home from a coffee-house the next May, which runs :—

"DEAR WIFE,—I hope I have done this day what will be pleasing to you ; in the meantime shall lie this night at a baker's, one leg over against the Devil Tavern, at Charing Cross. I shall be able to confront the fools who wish me uneasy, and shall have the satisfaction to see thee cheerful and at ease. If the printer's boy be at home, send him hither, and let Mrs. Todd send by the boy my night-gown, slippers and clean linen. You shall hear from me early in the morning," etc.

On April 12th, 1709, appeared quietly the first sheet of the Tatler, destined—it and its successors—to affect powerfully the manners of that time, and to open a new era in our literature. Though projected under the *alias* of Isaac Dickerstaff, the paper's real author was detected by Addison, reading it in Dublin, and that part of his own writings which possess for us the greatest value first came from his pen at the suggestion of his friend. The Tatler was issued on three mornings in the week, each pamphlet taking a subject illustrative of some of the light follies of the period, usually some comic incident supplied by the mind of the writer. Charming wit and good nature filled them all, and yet if in the midst of their enjoyment of the fun, the laughter of our patched or bewigged ancestors was suddenly broken by the idea that perhaps, after all, they were chuckling at themselves, the Essayist's true aim was gained Vanity was surprised into censure of itself. To the student of manners, Steele's unlaboured and lifelike papers are of great charm, as well as historical value. In the Spectator, the work was evenly shared with Addison, and became more pretentious. The writer was more a Spectator of mankind than one of the species, as he owns in the first sheet, and was more speculative than practical. He brought philosophy out of closets and libraries, schools and colleges, to dwell in clubs and assemblies, at tea-tables, and in coffee-houses. Hazlitt says that what Steele wrote "is more like the remarks which occur in sensible conversa- "tion, and less like a lecture. The indications of character and strokes of "humour are more true and frequent, the reflections that suggest themselves "arise from the occasion, and are less spun out into regular dissertations." Steele's love for the whole race was quite undisguised, and breathes from every line he wrote. It never left him, even in days when he was troubled by very poor health. He worshipped his wife and his friend, and would not be angry at the severe treatment he got from them both, sometimes. Writing of himself a few months after Addison's death, in his paper, the Theatre, he says : "There is not now in his sight that excellent man, whom Heaven made his friend and superior, to be at a certain place in pain for what he should say or do. I will go on in his further encouragement. The best woman that ever man had cannot now lament and pine at his neglect of himself." Despite the opposite temperaments of the two men, in more than one important respect they were alike. Their early and long friendship was due very much to the attraction of contrast, which is said to draw together the reserved and the jovial as to the oneness of their aim. They admired alike. They were both sincere men, religious, loving purity in thought, and simplicity in words. Some Essays of Steele are not to be known from those of the other by any analysis of expression. Without a signature, we should be quite in the dark for the true author. On the other side of the picture, Addison, we know, went at times as deep in his cups as the Irishman, who had not been born to deliberate. Had the two lived in our day, they would no doubt have confined themselves to tea and soda water, but the spirit of their age was too strong for them. They tried to bet er it in other respects, and the charming good humour with which they appealed to its best elements, shamed away part of its folly. But the world did not acknowledge their great worth until they were gone, and Steele is known to have died forgotten by it, many years after his friend.

A. G. P.

JONATHAN SWIFT.

If there be any truth in Mr. Forster's remark that it is impossible to form a just opinion of the *real* character of Jonathan Swift without a deep and thorough knowledge of his works and letters, it may appear presumptuous for one who cannot pretend to more than a very slight acquaintance with the subject, to say anything upon it at all. But there are certain facts in his history which cannot well be disputed, and certain features of his general character which are admitted by all.

It is a knotty point whether a man's birthplace stamps him as belonging to the nation within whose borders he first saw the light. Swift's father was of an old Yorkshire family which had done good service in the Royalist cause, and both his parents were born and bred in England. His father, who was in poor circumstances, had managed to get employment in Dublin. Here, in 1667, a month or two after his father's death, Swift was born, so that he was, undoubtedly, an Irishman as far as the fact of his birth in Ireland could make him so ; but it is claimed, on the other hand, that his education was begun in England, for his nurse carried him off to Whitehaven before he was a year old, and kept him there until he was three, so that he was able to read before he returned to the land of his birth. He seems to have taken little pains to make the best of what slight advantages he had in the way of education during the years his uncle Godwin kept him at an Irish school ; nor did he attempt to distinguish himself at the University of Dublin, where, in fact, the only branches of study to which he paid any attention were literature and history, neglecting all else to such an extent that he only obtained his degree by special grace, an inglorious but then not uncommon manner of gaining the necessary title. He remained in Dublin for a time, and on the breaking out of the troubles joined his mother, who had meantime returned to her native place. From her he went, about 1688, to live with Sir William Temple, in a position somewhat akin to that of secretary, a connection from which were woven into his life many threads destined to entwine themselves permanently with his very existence, and to affect him during the rest of his days. The families of Temple and Swift had of old been friends ; and the contact with the political world through Sir William was the first step towards elevating Jonathan Swift to the position of importance which he afterwards filled, and which he thought his due from the first moment we have any record of his feelings. One of his chief characteristics at this time seems to have been a morbid, passionate resentment against the cruel fate which had placed a man of his vast and brilliant abilities in so subservient and dependent a position ; this unhealthy frame of mind appears to have had a place in his nature from his earliest boyhood, completely casting out that spirit of humility or even contentment, which would have enabled him to accept his lot with patience, and in accepting it to utilize more fully the advantages which, though small, he might, with his enormous natural endowments, have turned to much greater advantage. Instead of going cheerfully to work and doing his best to rise by his own exertions to the position he thought himself worthy of, he sat still, taking what was offered him, with a spirit of thankless ingratitude, and cursing the day that he was born. He seems to have been entirely lacking in that manly spirit of independence which would never have allowed him to rest quiet under the feeling that he was relying on another for his very subsistence ; but he took what came to him, and lamented that it was not more ; that Providence did not at once exalt him to a station worthy of his own ideas, without his being obliged to make an effort to climb the ascent which separated his ideal from the despised reality. On the other hand, he was not ungenerous, but, with a thoroughly un-Irish spirit of liberality, he practised charity with calculation ; giving only where there was evident necessity, and where he could do real good ; but in such a case doing enough to accomplish the object he had in view. Nay, sometimes he gave with a spirit of true charity ; for his assistance was afforded in such a way that the recipient was either unaware whence it came, or was led to imagine that it was a right and not a favour. Though careful almost to meanness about unnecessary and personal expenses, he nevertheless was so ready to help where help was needed, that he died without having accumulated any great amount of money. It is impossible here to say much about his brilliant wit, and magnificent intellectual gifts, for they are so well-known ; even Johnson has allowed that no author can be found who has borrowed so little, or who has so well maintained his claim to be called original. Scott remarks, besides, that he excelled in every style of composition which he attempted.

But this is anticipating somewhat. To return to his life at Sir William Temple's and the influences at work upon him there. The present generation are often told by their elders that the race is degenerating, and that the fashionable modern complaints were unheard of in the good old days, not so long ago, when the world was happy and tranquil in the absence of rush and bustle, and the rapid interchange of ideas which characterize modern life since the introduction of steam, when people could not meet so often, and consequently had to talk about something better and more improving than their own feelings and sensations. But, speaking without medical accuracy on the subject, I may say that Swift contracted at Sir William Temple's a tendency to that malady which is now almost a necessity to modern civilized life, namely, dyspepsia. This may seem a small point to touch upon, but who can tell how great was the influence of this weakness of body upon his mind in after years. In a person of a disciplined, patient, thoughtful nature, a bodily trial such as this would exercise an ennobling, refining influence ; but with a man of Swift's disposition, already morbidly bitter in his resentment against the world for not having, of its own accord, allotted him the position he desired, it only added to his bitterness and lessened the chance of his becoming softened and reconciled to his lot.

There is another important feature of this period of his life which may be
mentioned. It is beside the purpose I have fixed for myself to-night to go into
his political life, which began practically at this season of his career with his
residence at Sir William Temple's. But then, also, he made the beginning of a
friendship which played a most important part in his literary as well as his private life, and it is, therefore, of great interest to us, for without it most of the
sources of our knowledge of his inner life and nature would have been lost to us.
It was there that he first met little Hester Johnson, of whose depth of affection
for him in after years there are so many touching proofs. His dear "Stella"
was but a child at the time, but her admiration and affection for him seem to
have dated from this period. Of this I shall say more later on.

After living about two years with Sir William Temple, Swift returned to Ireland for the benefit of his health ; but not attaining the end he desired, he went
back again to Sir William Temple's, which seems to have been more his home
during the middle portion of his life than any other place ; for we find him
returning there again and again, upon every fresh disappointment to which his
discontented nature subjected him. He was ordained to a prebend in the
North of Ireland in 1694, which he apparently took only as a means of preferment, for he gave it up as soon as he found that it led to nothing. He went
back again to Ireland in the anomalous position for a clergyman, of Secretary to
the Earl of Berkeley, who gave him a living which led to a better post of pre-
bendary in St. Patrick's Cathedral in Dublin ; this seems to have kept him quiet
for a time. But he did not give up his visits to England, and after a good deal
of manœuvering he succeeded in getting himself appointed Dean of St. Patrick's
in 1713. This was his highest dignity, for his enemies prevented his appointment to a bishopric, which, on one occasion, he nearly obtained. He had plenty
of enemies, for not only was he proud and haughty by nature, but his manners
to those from whom he expected nothing, were overbearing and insolent to a
degree.

The established facts as to the manner in which he obtained his prefer-
ments and political position do not lead one to think that there could have been
much depth of religious feeling about him ; but some who knew him intimately
assert that he scrupulously fulfilled the duties of his station in that respect,
both in public and in private; and it may be that his manner was in public
rough and course, because his very pride made him fear that men would consider
him a hypocrite if his pretensions seemed higher than his way of life. Many a
man fails to conform himself in his outward behaviour, even to his own stand-
ard, lest the world should think him Pharisaical. But there is certainly reason
to fear that Swift was not essentially superior to the men with whom he associated ; for he betrays himself by sins of commission if not of omission ; some
of his writings are coarse and disgusting to a degree that would render them un-
fit for a place in modern literature. His apologists would have us believe that
his splendid wit was only thus used for a good end, and that his immense power
of satire must be allowed to run a little beyond ordinary limits, and to follow

the fashion of the day ; but though we may admit that natural wit and humour may be turned to good use even in support of the cause of religion, yet sure'y the same cannot be said of degrading and sensual coarseness. Some of the more charitable of his biographers wish to prove that he was mad from his birth, but this is not generally allowed, though few would like to say how little it takes to overbalance the mind of a great genius.

I fear I have exceeded my limit of time already, but my sketch would be too incomplete without a few words on Swift's loves. If he ever experienced the feeling of true love, it was for his dear Stella, who certainly gave him her whole heart ; but his treatment of her is much more rationally explained by thinking that his pride was more touched by her unflagging admiration, than his love kindled by her whole-hearted devotion. That he admired and appreciated her intellect, as well as the charms of her person, cannot be doubted ; but his cold and calculating nature would not easily give itself up to unconditional love. She had come to Ireland with an aunt, at his suggestion, after Sir William Temple's death, and was constantly in his society. But he never seems to have desired more than the Platonic love which her nearness enabled him to gratify, and there is melancholy evidence that the want of responsive feeling on his part hastened her death, by the weight of suspense and uncertainty which it threw upon her. This was not the only part of his behaviour towards her for which we blame him. During one of his long absences in England, he became acquainted with a lady named Vanhomrigh, whose eldest daughter, Esther, seems to have been unable to resist the powerful attraction of Swift's wonderful intellect, and gave herself up to love for him without any open seeking for it on his part. He found their house very pleasant, and his visits became frequent ; for "Vanessa," as he calls her, proved an apt pupil, whose ready homage was so pleasing to Swift's vanity, that he disregarded the danger to her for the sake of his own enjoyment, and allowed her affections to develop unchecked. His Journal to Stella, which had been up to this time a complete outpouring of all his thoughts and desires, became constrained ; and it is only in reply to a direct question that he informs her of the intimacy with the Vanhomrighs. At last Vanessa's ardent passion overstepped the conventional restraints, and she openly avowed her love, only to discover that she had failed to awaken a corresponding sentiment in Swift's breast. But she was not to be put off, and followed him to Ireland, where her unhappy end was hastened by despair when she found that if Swift had in his composition any of the affection she desired, it was felt only for Stella. The news of the latter's marriage is said to have been the last straw which broke her down completely. This is partly conjecture, for it is thought by some that Swift never married at all, and certainly it is a point involved in much obscurity. If he did marry Stella he was too selfish to own it publicly, and even when she was dying, broken down by the sorrow and anxiety which his behaviour had caused her, he kept away, and deprived her of the only comfort which it was in the power of mortal to bestow in her last hours.

His own end was very melancholy. He felt his powers failing, and compared himself to a tree whose boughs had been shattered by lightning, saying, "I shall be like that tree, I shall die first at the top." These words were most painfully fulfilled, for he sank into a condition of idiocy from which he never recovered, but failed gradually, until at last in 1745, he was mercifully released from an existence which was merely an existence to him, and only a trial to others.

DANIEL DE FOE.

Daniel Foe, born in London in 1661. was the son of a well-to-do butcher, named James Foe, who lived in the parish of St. Giles, Cripplegate. His humble origin perhaps accounts for the sentiments expressed by him in The True-born Englishman. " Then let us boast of ancestors no more, for fame of families is all a cheat ; 'Tis personal virtue only makes us great." It was not until he was about the age of forty that he changed his name to Defoe ; why he did so, does not seem to have been found out, but it was probably to distinguish himself from his father, who was known to his friends as Mr. Foe. He came of a Dissenting family and was educated at a Dissenting Academy kept by Charles Morton at Newington Green. In consequence of this he was often taunted with what seems to have been an unfounded charge, that of being an uneducated man. This he always bitterly resented and once replied to Swift, who had spoken of him as " an illiterate fellow whose name I forget," that " he had been in his time pretty well master of five languages, and had not lost them yet, though he wrote no bill at his door, nor set Latin quotations on the front of the *Review.*" His first pamphlet seems to have been written in 1683, at the age of twenty-one years, though no copy of it has been found. In 1685, he took up arms for the Duke of Monmouth and on the defeat of that nobleman was fortunate enough to escape the clutches of Judge Jeffreys and Kirke's Lambs, although three of his former fellow students at Newington were hanged. He then took up the more peaceful occupation of a hosier in Freeman's Court, Cornhill, and from a passage in his Complete English Tradesman we gather that his business occasionally took him to Spain. After seven years, in 1692, he was obliged to flee from his creditors to Bristol, but managed, as he boasted, to finally pay them off. There is a story told of him that he was known as the Sunday Gentleman while there, because he appeared on that day only and in fashionable attire, being kept indoors the rest of the week by the bailiffs. During the reign of James II., he, in all probability, wrote other pamphlets but put his name to none.

On the accession of William in 1688 he became, and always continued to be, a strenuous supporter of that King " of glorious memory" and was one of a volunteer regiment composed of the chief citizens and commanded by the celebrated Earl of Peterborough, which attended the King and Queen to the Mansion House in 1689. Three years afterwards he wrote the first pamphlet which we know for certain was his ;— A new discovery of an Old Intrigue, a Satire levelled at Treachery and Ambition. He wrote several other pamphlets in favour of William and was rewarded by being appointed Accountant to the Commissioners of the Glass Duty, which office he held till the duty was abolished in 1699. About this time he set up a manufactory of bricks and pan-tiles at Tilbury in which he seems to have prospered, as he set up a carriage and a pleasure boat. His pamphlet in favour of a standing army came rather late, as the question had been pretty well decided by that time, but he boasted in his preface that " if books and writings would not, God be thanked the Parliament would confute" his adversaries, a sentiment which, when in after years, it was applied to himself he did not perhaps admire so much. Mr. Minto says : " None of his subsequent tracts surpass this as a piece of trenchant and persuasive reasoning. It shows at their very highest his marvellous powers of combining constructive with destructive criticism.... He makes no parade of logic ; he is only a plain freeholder like the mass whom he addresses, though he knows twenty times as much as many writers of more pretension... He wrote for a class to whom a prolonged intellectual operation, however comprehensive and complete, was distateful."

At this time (1701) there was a great deal of feeling in England against William favouring his Dutch fellow-countrymen, and this was brought to a climax by Tutchin, an old enemy of Defoe, publishing " a vile pamphlet in abhorred verses entitled The Foreigners." Defoe retorted in defence of William by his celebrated pamphlet The True-born Englishman in which he somewhat unpatriotically describes the English as the most mongrel race that ever lived on the face of the earth. " For Englishmen to boast of generation, Cancels their knowledge, and lampoons the nation, A true-born Englishman's a contradiction, In speech an irony, in fact a fiction." This production, though contrary to popular prejudice at the time, was very successful, 80,000 copies of it being sold on the streets. It also brought Defoe into the King's personal favour which advantage however was brief, as William died about a year after.

Defoe first broke with the Dissenters by writing against Occasional Conformity thus placing them in a dilemma which they did not relish and bringing persecution upon them, nor did he improve matters by telling them that forbidding the practice of Occasional Conformity would do them good by ridding them of lukewarm adherents. All those who held public offices were obliged to conform to the rites of the Church of England and the Dissenters avoided this by occasionally going to the Established Church and attending their own Church at other times. When the Bill against Occasional Conformity was brought into the House of Commons, the Dissenters resented Defoe's writing bitterly, as showing the enemy where to strike. When, however, after passing the Commons, the Bill was opposed in the Lords, Defoe suddenly changed about and published his most famous pamphlet. The Shortest Way with the Dissenters, which was intended, as he said *afterwards*, as banter on the High flying Tory Churchmen, and not as bearing on the Occasional Conformity Bill at all. This was not at first recognized as a satire, and a Cambridge fellow thanked his bookseller for having sent him so excellent a treatise—next to the Holy Bible and the Sacred Comments the most valuable he had seen. Great was the wrath of the Church party when it was discovered to be a satire on themselves nor were the Dissenters much reassured when they found the proposal was not serious. He was indicted, fined, and sentenced to stand three times in the pillory ; the Shortest Way was burnt by the hangman. Contrary to their usual custom the crowd, instead of garbage, threw bunches of flowers at the prisoner and drank to his health. Their enthusiasm was increased by his Hymn to the Pillory ; in which he says of those who put him there : " Tell 'em the men who plac'd him here, are friends unto the times. But at a loss to find his guilt, they can't commit his crimes." He was not released from Newgate till August 1704, and it was in that prison that he began his Review. Through Harley's influence he was set free, according to his own account, on condition that he should keep silence for seven years. In reality however he was taken into the service of the government.

Defoe was no longer the straightforward advocate of King William's policy. He was engaged henceforward in serving two masters, persuading each that he served him alone, and persuading the public, in spite of numberless insinuations, that he served nobody but them and himself, and wrote simply as a free lance under the jealous sufferance of the Government of the day. He used all his influence to favour the Treaty of Union, living for some time in Edinburgh. The suspicion was very freely expressed that while there he was acting as the agent, if not as the spy, of the government, and though he denied it most strenuously at the time, he afterwards admitted that he was acting as an agent of Harley. " When he was despatched on secret missions he could depart wiping his eyes at the hardship of having to flee from his creditors." On Harley's fall from the ministry he went over to Godolphin on the plea of maintaining at any cost the public credit, which at that time was very low. He admitted his difficulty, and said, " If a man could be found that could sail North and South, that could speak truth and falsehood, that could turn to the right hand and the left all at the same time, he would be the man that should now speak" After 1715 Defoe ceased to take part in the contraversies of the times in the way in which he had done during his previous life, but owing to the exertions of Mr. Lee, many works of his have been found since then, he having written for at least seven periodical publications. In April 1719, he made a new departure, and published his Robinson Crusoe, which met with such sudden popularity that the purchaser of the manuscript is said to have made £1000 by it, and it is not too much to say of this work which surpasses any of his subsequent novels, that but for it his name would have been unknown in our day except to students of History. Finding he had hit on a profitable business, Defoe wrote about ten other large works after this, among which, in 1722, The Plague of London. He died in poverty and on not very good terms with his family and the rest of the world. Professor Morley says " with Defoe we begin the renewal of a race of greater men, who dealt with essentials of life as all true thinkers do. They spoke straight home to the main body of the people, created by degrees a more national audience and wrote under influence of a sense they had to touch the minds and hearts of Englishmen at large. Their matter rose in worth, their manner became more direct, and there was a gradual paling of French classical moonshine in the dawn of what may be called an English Popular Influence." A recent biographer says of him. " He was a great, a truly great, liar, perhaps the greatest liar that ever lived. His dishonesty went too deep to be called superficial, yet, if we go deeper still in his rich and strangely mixed nature, we come upon stubborn foundations of con-science... Shifty as Defoe was, and admirably as he used his genius for circum-stantial invention to cover his designs, there was no other statesman of his generation who remained more true to the principle of the Revolution, and to the cause of civil and religious freedom." Though in many of two hundred and fifty works he treats of high and lofty aims we do not think that he himself believed that " there is but one work worthy of a man, the production of a truth, to which we devote ourselves, and in which we believe."

W. W. R.

PASTORAL POETRY.

EDWARD KIRKE, in his introduction to Spenser's Shepheardes Calender says, that the new and then unknown poet had begun with Eclogues, "following the example of the best and most ancient poets, who devised this kind of writing, being so base for the matter, and homely for the manner, at the first to try their abilities."

The Eclogue is one of the three divisions of Pastoral Poetry, the other two being the Bucolic and the Idyll. These terms, however, so overlap one another in meaning, that it is difficult to distinguish between them.

Spenser insists on deriving the word Eclogue from the Greek "Aigon Logoi," tales concerning goats, and says in defence of his position, that Theocritus, being the nearest to the source of Pastoral Poetry, is the best authority; and that he uses Eclogue in this sense, making most of his speakers, goatherds.

The common derivation, is from the Greek word, ekloge, signifying choice, and the title has come to mean, "a small elegant composition written in a simple and natural manner. It differs from the Idyll, (a word taken from the Greek Eidullion, Latin Idyllium, meaning a little form or image), only in the fact that shepherds are usually introduced as conversing in the Eclogue, and not in the Idyll. This, however, is a modern distinction, for Theocritus calls his pastorals, which are often dialogues, Idyllia.

The third term, the Bucolic, must also have signified nearly the same thing as Eclogue in old times, for Virgil divides his Bucolics into Eclogues, but afterwards, it must have been applied chiefly to one kind of comedy, for Vossius thought it necessary to distinguish it from the latter, by saying that while both describe ordinary affairs, Comedy represents the manners of city people—Bucolics those of country people. A further examination will show that Bucolics may consist of action alone, narration alone; or, again, of both, and that their forms may be either monologue or dialogue.

What is still to be learned of the nature of Pastoral Poetry, may perhaps best be gathered from a sketch of its history, from its source down to the Elizabethan era, for which a few words must suffice.

Origin. The origin of this kind of composition has called forth much diversity of opinion. One has traced it to Orpheus, another has made Pastorals co-eval with the world itself; but we "should not naturally expect to find the unobtrusive occupation of the Shepherd attracting the attention of any unrefined mind," and there is no good reason for dating the origin of the Pastoral from any earlier period than that of Theocritus, many of whose poems have come down to us. In his days, about 275 B. C., the people of Sicily had attained to a great degree of civilization.

The works of Theocritus are results of accurate observation, and as they copy the manners and the subjects of the description, we find in them, at different times, both rude and elegant simplicity. The great beauty of Sicily and the opportunities afforded by foreign travel gave Theocritus every advantage in describing natural scenery.

His Idyllia are, so far as we know, the only original Pastorals, for, in form at least, all subsequent poets in this line, from Virgil to Philips, are mere copyists.

Two other men, Bion and Moschus, might be mentioned with Theocritus. Moschus lived in Syracuse, and both were contemporary with Theocritus, but they were not such purely Pastoral poets. Among the Latins, Virgil and Ausonius both wrote Idylls, but the name with them was of wider signification than among the Greeks.

Modern Times. In modern times, the Idyll was revived by the Provençal poets, and especially by Regnier, but it is to *Italy*, its ancient home, that we must look for the sources of that impulse, which, passing through France, reached England about A. D. 1500. Boccaccio, in his Admeto, sounded the first note, which was taken up by Agnolo Poliziano, (1450), who, educated at the expense of Cosmo de' Medici, became Greek and Latin Professor at Florence. "A poet as well as teacher," he has left us the first Pastoral (under the title of Orfeo), with a connected story, to be found in modern literature.

During the following years, many other pieces appeared as Pastoral Eclogues, Rustic Comedies, etc. ; but the most important work of[this kind was published in 1504. This was the "Arcadia" of Sanazzaro, which contains twelve Eclogues, each with a preface in prose. This work was written in Latin. The growing taste for Pastoral poetry, as well as the popularity of the authors, is shown by the fact, that sixty editions were published during the century. The Italian influence on *Spain*, then paramount, was shown afresh in the Pastorals of Garcilasso de la Vega, the only Spanish author who attained any eminence in this style, and that it spread as far as *Portugal*, was evidenced by the imitation of Sanazzaro's work, published shortly after, by George of Monte Mayor.

In *France*, in the time of Francis I, Clement Marot wrote Pastorals, which he converted into religious pieces, showing sympathy with the reformers of the Church. In this respect he was followed by Spenser. The Shepherdes Calender was not, however, the first Pastoral written in English. That was left to us by Robert Henryson, when he died about the year 1500, and was named Robene and Makyue. This production "shows much simple and natural beauty, and underlying religious earnestness."

It is noticeable, as showing that the revival of the Pastoral was a result of the new attention now given to the Classics, that Greek was first taught in Oxford shortly before this, by William Grocyn, and Henryson himself had compiled into elegant and ornamental metre, The Morall Fables of Æsope, the Phrygian.

Respecting the rise of Pastoral Poetry in England, Taine says, that, contemporary with Sidney, there arose a great multitude of poets, indicating an extraordinary condition of the national mind. Men had no theories but new senses. They saw what is hidden from common eyes ; they saw the soul in all things, and felt within themselves the sad or delicious sentiment that breathes from a combination or union, like a harmony or a cry. They "saw an air of resignation in trees, felt the feverish tumult of the waves."   *   *   *
"Only a step further is needed, and the old gods reappear, and all the splendour and sweetness of nature assembles round them."

The rich sunny country, and gods and goddesses as impersonations of grace and strength, are objects fitted to give joy, and we find them in abundance in the poetry of the time, whether taking the form of Sonnets or Pastorals, some of which are so lovely, delicate and easily unfolded, that we have nothing to compare with them, since like Theocritus and Moschus, these poets play with their smiling gods and goddesses. Where the power of embellishment was so great, it was natural that they should also paint ideal love, the sentiment which unites all joys, especially artless and happy love, made up of innocence, self-abandonment, and devoid of reflection and effort.

Spenser's Shepherdes Calender is a thought-inspiring and tender pastoral, full of delicate loves, noble sorrows, lofty ideas, where no voice is heard but of thinkers and poets : gods, men, landscapes, the world which he sets in motion, is a thousand miles away from that in which we live."

E. R. B.

NOTE.—The principal English pastorals, written since Spenser's time, are Milton's Minor Poems, Pope's Windsor Forest, Thomson's Seasons, and Goldsmith's Deserted Village.

ALEXANDER POPE.

On the 21st of May, 1688, in Lombard Street, London, was born Alexander Pope. A coruscation of the age in which he lived, it had been strange had this man been produced elsewhere than in the intense focus of the ideas, business, and somewhat corrupt civilization of his time. To trace through several generations the chain of being which pronounced itself eventually in a Pope would be a most interesting study in mental physiology—or, perhaps, more properly speaking—pathology. As we cannot do this, however, and know little of real importance, even with regard to his parents, it may suffice to state that his father was classified with respect to his method of bread-winning as a linen merchant, that he retired early from business with a competence to Binfield, in the neighbourhood of Windsor Forest, and there devoted himself to his garden and the care of his only child. Pope's parents were Roman Catholics, and therefore somewhat cut off from the busy life of the day, but doubtless yet near enough to feel powerfully its reflex action. Young Pope, a home-bred boy, sickly, weak, precocious, may be supposed to have developed first in an atmosphere more or less morbid, an eddy or backwater to the current of his time, nimble in proportion to its force. He missed that early contact and attrition with others which a public school might have afforded, which rubs off the poor edges and sharp angles, and produces a stately, self-confident man of the world, who, with the ordinary worldly objects in view, is content to follow the beaten track and even tenor of his way toward them. Pope's mind, developing rapidly, crystallized in a finer, more fragile and peculiar form. It may depend on the turning of a straw whether such a nature, united, in Pope's case, with physical weakness, may tread mentally and morally downward or upward through life, reaching, perhaps, heights or depths seldom attained. There is scarcely room for that free interaction of influence which leads to the soft middle course ; the mind yields to one dominant idea. Intellectually, Pope, without becoming a Homer or a Shakespeare, achieved a facility, polish, and culture in verse seldom reached by others. But morally, instead of becoming a saint, he appears to have been a rebel against whatever of formulated good characterized his age, to have said to himself, like the Duke of Gloucester in Richard the Third—" I that am curtailed of this fair proportion, Cheated of feature by dissembling nature, Deformed, unfinished, sent before my time Into this breathing world scarce half-made up.... I am determined to prove a villain And hate the idle pleasures of those days."

To follow Pope's career in detail is, at this date, a matter of little interest. To the catalogue of his works and the dates of their publication might be added the chronicle of appreciation, praise, detraction, calumny, even abuse, which in proportion to his prominence he received in due measure. From a very early age books became his delight ; he read Dryden's works, and came personally in contact with the aged poet, who, it has been remarked, "could hardly have looked at the delicate and deformed boy, whose preternatural acuteness and sensibility were seen in his dark eyes, without a feeling approaching to grief had he known that he was to fight a battle like that under which he was himself then sinking, even though the Temple of Fame should at length open to receive him." His biographers are constantly reminding one of his extraordinary precocity. At twelve he wrote the Ode to Solitude, concluding—

> " Thus let me live, unseen, unknown,
> Thus unlamented let me die,
> Steal from the world, and not a stone
> Tell where I lie."

This is surely a strange subject or sentiment for a boy, but Pope was never a boy. At sixteen he wrote the Pastorals (of which more anon) and part of Windsor Forest, and about this time, taken with a new whim, imagined himself dying, and wrote farewell letters to his friends. His malady proved, however, to lie within the remedial influence of good advice and exercise. At twenty-three he produced his Essay on Criticism, an effort proving his full maturity of mind, and in the same year printed The Rape of the Lock. Two years later he began a six years' task in the translation of Homer's Iliad, and in 1722 undertook the Odyssey, paying assistants, however, to help him in this work, and selling the copyright for a good sum. In 1727 appeared the Dunciad, and in 1732 the first epistle of the Essay on Man, and so proved his life filled with multiplying colours to the end.

In his early literary days Pope was much in London, and had a part in the coarser pleasures of that city, but at the age of twenty-seven he returned to Twickenham, living there in comparative retirement to the end of his days. Yet he was by no means a recluse, but came in contact with most of the wits and poets of his time, including Swift, Gay, and even Voltaire. He suffered keenly under adverse criticism, though endeavouring to conceal his feelings, but concentrated all his powers of satire, irony, and invective in the Dunciad, in which he took full vengeance on his critics. It is said that "some were stricken mad with rage, others dumb with consternation, some fled for refuge to ale, others to ink, while not a few fell or feared to fall into the jaws of famine.."

Pope, it was said, "could not drink tea without a stratagem," and was singularly devoid of conscientiousness and truth. Witness the discreditable and foolish trickery practised in the matter of the publication of his correspondence, for there seems little doubt that the whole affair was got up to mystify the public and arouse curiosity—a ruse altogether unworthy of a mind so keen and clear, but quite in harmony its jealous and warped character.

In May, 1744, at the age of fifty-six, Pope died, "tired of the world," a nominal Catholic, but in truth without belief. " There is nothing meritorious," he said with his last breath, "but virtue and friendship, and, indeed, friendship itself is only a part of virtue."

A word or two on Pope's genius and style. It cannot be denied that Pope was a true poet, and, if popular appreciation be any criterion of this, it is probable that more pointed sayings of Pope have become common property than of any other poets save Shakespeare and Young. To make a great poet, however, two powers are required in combination, the perceptive or appreciative, and the conceptive or idealistic. In the first of these Pope was singularly strong, in the second peculiarly weak. He could describe and embalm in neat, polished, flowing verse, any object from the most trivial to the greatest—every word fitly chosen, every period carefully studied, his very manuscripts evidencing by their corrections and recorrections the elaborateness of his work. Thoroughly artificial, he could adopt easily, and wear gracefully, the Classical dress which ill became the other English poets of the Eighteenth century. Gilfillan writes, "You would say of Pope, 'He smells of the midnight lamp,' not as of Dante, of whom the boys cried out on the street, 'Lo! the man that was in hell.'" He wants in original as in sublime thought, but nimbly clothes the teeming fancies of his mind in the most becoming and appropriate garb. He is related to Shakespeare, Milton, or Chaucer, as is an accomplished gallant to an ardent lover, provided for every occasion with an appropriate expression or fitting gesture ; he simulates *better* than the life ; he escapes those bluntnesses into which the very earnestness of the other may lead him. Pope's mind may be compared to a polished and perfect mirror, reflecting truly and minutely each object on which it turned, but adding nothing. He is an illustrious example of the point which pure art may reach when unendowed with the heaven-descended gift of imagination. The ideal is wanting in his poetry, the power which, emanating from the poet's mind, breathes the breath of life into his objects and raises even the meanest into a fitting emblem of some divine truth. In many of his poems we find an admiration-compelling Arabesque, but, when the novelty has passed away, turn with relief to the few suggestive master-strokes by which a truer artist represents his ideal. To quote again from Gilfillan, " Keats would have comprised all the poetry of ' Windsor Forest ' in one sonnet or line ; indeed, has he not done so, where, describing his soul following the note of the nightingale into the far depths of the woods, where she is pouring out her heart in song, he says—

" And with thee fade away into the forest dim."

His renderings of Homer are not so much translations as transmutations, in which he dresses the Odyssey and Iliad in the costume of his time. He strews flowers along the paths of the stern old heroes, tips their spears with tinsel, and reduces the very blood which flows from their wounds to a colourless ichor. Pope's Pastorals, with which we are more immediately concerned this evening, appear to be an attempt to clothe ever-living feelings and sentiments in the masquerade costumes of a bygone age. Of these it has been said with, perhaps, undue severity, that, "like all well finished commonphrases, they were received with instant and unusual applause." G. D.

POPE'S MORAL ESSAYS.

As a sketch of Pope's life has already been given, I shall confine my remarks, this evening, to the subject of the works that are to be read, and judge of them by what they profess to be ; — *Moral Essays*. Unlike the Pastorals, the product of an immature mind of sixteen, they were written in Pope's later years, and immediately after the Essay on Man. The first, on the Use of Riches, appeared in the same year, 1733, and the Characters of Men and Women in the following year. The Essay on Man was originally intended to have been a much larger work, and to have consisted of four books ; the first, as it considers man in the abstract and in every one of his relations, was to be the foundation of the whole ; the other three parts, the superstructure to be raised upon that. The second was to treat of Man in his intellectual capacity at large ; the third, Man in his social, political, and religious aspect, and the fourth was to treat of Practical Morality, of which the four Essays we have before us to-night were to be an illustration. The two first, on the Characters of Men and Women, were the introductory part of the concluding book. This was the author's favourite work. He had given it long and serious attention. It was intended to have been the only work of his riper years, but for some reasons, best known to himself, he never carried out his intentions, and instead of four books as the Essay of Man, we have but one, and the Moral Essays as a detached poem. As they are so closely connected, I shall not consider it foreign to the subject to devote a little time to the Essay itself. It appeared at first without a name. The report had gone abroad, it is true, that Pope was busy on a system of Morality. He took care to send it, before publication, to those authors whom he had already offended, and who were suspected of ill-will towards him, that the praises they would lavish upon it, might not be withdrawn when the author's name became known. Also the friends of Pope, who were in the secret, were very busy, everywhere, lauding the excellence of the poem, fearing Pope would henceforth meet a dangerous rival. After the second and third Epistles were finished, he acknowledged the fourth, and claimed the honour of a Moral Poet. Let us stop a moment to ask whence the claim to such an honour? His own ideas on religious subject were so shadowy and unreal that his friend, Lord Bolingbroke, could inspire him with much of his metaphysical and atheistical philosophy without his knowing it. When translated into French it was attacked by Crousaz, a Swiss Professor, on the ground of its antagonism to Revelation, and its tendency to fatalism. Warburton, unasked, came forward in its defence, and Pope acknowledged, " you understand my system better than I do myself." In fact, it is utterly without a system—an ingenious puzzle, that makes " confusion worse confounded." Let us give a passing glance at a few passages. He sets out " to vindicate the ways of God to man." What are some of those ways ?

> " Who knows, but He whose hand the lightning forms,
> Who heaves old Ocean, and wings the storms ;
> Pours fierce ambition in a Cæsar's mind,
> Or turns young Ammon loose to scourge mankind ?
> From pride, from pride, our very reas'ning springs,
> Account for moral, as for nat'ral things ;
> Why charge we Heav'n in those, in these acquit ?
> In both to reason right is to submit."

Here, then, are some of God's ways ; the evil men do, fierce ambition —the cruelty which makes men the scourges of mankind, are like the storms in the natural world—the direct work of God—the author of Evil as of Good. The same confusion of thought runs through the whole, more or less, as he repeats more than once, " whatever is—is right." If I undertake to describe a person's ways, I must surely understand somewhat of that person's character. I cannot vindicate the ways of a man, unless I know the man himself. Pope undertakes to do in the first epistle what in the second he confesses no man able to do, when he says :—

> " Know then thyself, presume not God to scan,
> The proper study of mankind is man."

And yet, with this acknowledged ignorance, he goes back again and again to the subject only to prove that he is "darkening counsel by words without knowledge."

The fact is, the age in which Pope lived was artificial and utterly skeptical. The English infidels, the precursors of the French skeptics of the last century, held undivided sway over all the cultivated minds of the period. The leading man amongst them was Pope's friend, Lord Bolingbroke, whom he apostrophizes in this Essay as " his genius, master of the poet and the song," his "guide, philosopher, and friend." Let a sentence, perhaps there is no sadder in the lan. guage, from Butler's preface to his great defence of revealed religion, show us how this moral pestilence had swept over the land, carrying death everywhere in its train. "It is come, I know not how, to be taken for granted, by many persons, that Christianity is not so much as a subject of enquiry ; but that it is now, at length, discovered to be fictitious. And accordingly they treat it, as if in the present age, this were an agreed point among all people of discernment, and nothing remained but to set it up as a principal subject of mirth and ridi- cule, as it were by way of reprisals, for its having so long interrupted the pleasures of the world."

Let us look, by way of contrast, to those words of deep pathos and beauty which Shakespeare puts into the mouth of Isabella, as she pleads for the life of her brother :—

" Alas, alas,
Why, all the souls that were, were forfeit once ;
And he that might the 'vantage best have took
Found out the remedy. How would you be
If He, which is the top of judgment, should
But judge you as you are ? O think of that
And mercy then will breathe within your lips
Like man new-made."

This blows like a healthy breeze over a plague-stricken land. We turn to it with delight, for in all the Essay there is neither a living God nor a living soul of man, nothing that breathes hope, and joy, and consolation into the troubled heart of man. Death—spiritual death is there, garnished and adorned it is true—sometimes by beautiful imagery—smooth couplets—easy, graceful verse —but underneath the clothing is only death. The man that Pope creates, I might rather say, tries to galvanize into life, has but two principles, Self-love and Reason, the one to urge, the other to restrain. Under the head of Self-love he describes the passions ; and anticipates what he brings out in the Characters of Men about the Ruling Passion, showing how closely they are connected, and how the first was to form the foundation of all that was to come after.

Now, let us see how Pope describes the characters of men. He acknowledges the difficulties of the subject. He argues that neither from Books, nor from Observation, nor from what reason may deduce from both, can we know what man is for he not only differs from others, but he differs from himself, under varying circumstances, and at different times. He then goes on to show the mistakes of philosophers who judge men by their deeds. The same actions may spring from very different motives, the motive and the action may be utterly unlike. A very trifling cause may lead to a very important event, so how can the sage be right in his conclusions ? Then the man of the world passes under censure, who judges men by their station, education, or opinions. Station gives a false colouring to the man. Education remodels him, so that his real nature is not known, and opinions are no guide, for they change with the changing tide.

He then brings forward what he believes to be the only key which unlocks the secret—the Ruling Passion—and portrays it in all its variety of working, and under every garb it may assume—strong in life—strong in death, and here the poet well describes it in the actress, the courtier, the miser, and the patriot.

But will this key fit every lock ? Have all, or even have most men a ruling passion ? We cannot think so. It is a coarse, rough way of meeting the difficulty. The fact is, Pope's standpoint is from without, not from within. It is a superficial view he takes. He sees not the great underlying principles which actuate all alike, though in such various form and degree. He sees not the essential oneness of the human heart, its endless diversity in unity. " He fashioneth their hearts alike." Like the human face, which reflects it, the same features are always present, but what a wonderful variety of form and expression.

When Massillon, the great French preacher, was asked how he, who was shut out from the world by his vows as a priest, could paint such life-like pictures of the passions of men, above all, of their self-love, he replied, "It is from the study of my own heart, that I derive the power of reading the hearts of others." Pope, on the other hand, held up a moral looking-glass, and that a distorted one, before his fellows, that he might behold their defects, and gloat over the horrid picture. Never did he look into that glass himself, for a faithful reflection of his own moral nature. Had he ever done so, he might have been a humbler and a wiser man, and have looked with a kindlier eye upon the failings of others.

And now what about his characters of women ? Has Pope been more happy in his pictures of them ?

> " Nothing so true as what you once let fall,
> Most women have no characters at all ;"

are the opening words of his Epistle. We feel inclined to answer in the words of Shakespeare—

> " Who steals my purse steals trash—'tis something, nothing,
> 'Twas mine, 'tis his, and has been slave to thousands ;
> But he that filches from me my good name,
> Robs me of that which not enriches him
> And makes me poor indeed."

After striving to picture these characterless women, he brings before us one who certainly had character enough, and who stands out prominently in the history of the times, Sarah, Duchess of Marlborough, under the name of Atossa. It is a powerful satire, and Pope was afraid to publish it till after her death. As in the characters of men, so here again he takes refuge in the thought of the Master Passion, only with this difference, that while men have many, women have but two loves—the love of pleasure and the love of sway.

Pope has no high ideal before him, no thought of woman's true position as an help-meet for man, to cheer him in his sadder hours, to inspire hope when clouds are gathering, with ready tact to clear a way through every difficulty, and with a strong love to smooth all the roughnesses of life.

Why Pope should have chosen such a subject as Moral Philosophy at all, with the idea that he was able to write upon it, we cannot tell. Was it that the Goddess of Revenge inspired him with the desire, in order that all unconsciously to himself he might appear at the head of the list of "dunces" he had lashed so mercilessly in his Dunciad, and that out of his own mouth posterity might ratify the sentence ?

If the spirit of Pope is with us to-night, I can fancy I hear the words —

" Fools rush in where angels fear to tread."

I meekly bow to the sentence, and now leave his angel friends to tread with a softer and more reverent step over the fields of his philosophy.

E. H. L.

PHILOSOPHY AND POPE.

As the student of philosophy traces his path through the ideas of others, he soon becomes aware that each thinker is endeavouring to frame a system for himself by one of two methods. If we speak of these methods in plain Saxon words, we may call them the *inward* and the *outward;* if we prefer to speak of them in better known philosophical terms, the method *a priori* and the method *a posteriori*. The *a priori* method is often known as the *subjective* method ; the method *a posteriori* as the *objective*. Now, it is evident that in old times, when observation and experiment, the two great engines of the *a posteriori* method, scarcely existed, the philosopher sought by inspection the true relations between himself and his fellows, himself and Nature, himself and an unknown, unseen power which controlled the universe. If acting thus, he discovered what he deemed an eternal verity, then everything, without more ado, was made wholly subservient to it, *subjective* as it was. The stars must move in the most perfect figure, said the *a priori* philosopher ; the most perfect figure is a circle ; therefore the stars move in a circle. This is a fair and actual specimen of such reasoning, applied to a phenomenon of the physical world. The stars may or may not move in a circle—that is of little moment to us ; but the fallacy is glaring as it stands. *The stars must move in the most perfect figure.* Why ? Because you imagine this to be the divine fitness of things ? How do you know that a circle *is* the most perfect figure, to begin with ; and again, suppose it were, what reason have you, except a prejudice in favour of circles, for your statement ? Then comes the *a posteriori*, the outward, the objective philosopher, and he commences by ascertaining a series of points in the paths of stars, and pronounces accordingly. Now, in regard to modern philosophy, the *a posteriori* method is paramount. To-day, philosophy, or let us rather speak of that branch of philosophy which deals with the individual mind, psychology, pre-supposes a fair knowledge of physiology as a reliable basis: The battle no longer ranges between the two methods, as a whole. It confines itself to the solution of this question : How far, up to what height, is the *a posteriori* method valid ?

The Eighteenth century is, in more respects than one, the period at which these matters were brought into striking contrast. Their forms then were not as they are now ; the protest against the extravaganzas into which the *a priori* thinker often suffered himself to be led, did not assume the sharp, clear, markedly defined procedure of the modern scientist, but still there was a protest. We see the germs of which the Nineteenth century exhibits the flower, as yet only partly unfolded. One proof of this is that the greatest landmark of the history of thought was set up not much more than one hundred and fifty years ago—the separation of Theology from Philosophy. In the ancient world such philosophy as existed was bound up tightiy in the bonds of theology ; such theology as existed, was supposed to contain all that was needful of philosophy. This remark of general character is true, in great measure, of Greek and Roman thought, but it especially applies to the Schoolmen. The later development, already hinted at, follows naturally. When *a posteriori* workers showed *a priori* speculators to be unsafe in certain particulars, amenable to experiment and observation, they would deny the validity of the *a priori* method in other particulars, not amenable ; would declare that it was unsafe in reference to things presumably higher and more mystic. In short, Scepticism and Infidelity arose.

Regarded from a *literary* standpoint, the Eighteenth century was remarkable for two reasons. First, the age of patronage was slowly dying away ; men could afford to take note of popular thought, to deal with it, to write for it. The need of pleasing an individual or a set of friends had disappeared. The second feature was that England seemed in every way subservient to French speculation and to French modes and habits of life. It may also be asserted that the Eighteenth century, compared with those that preceded, no less than with those that followed it, was one of intellectual repose. The discordant elements which bid fair to work on society like leaven, producing a new and altogether strange condition. were hushed by compromise. No lasting quiet could be ensured, it is true ; but many of the combatants laid their weapons at their feet so as to be ready in case of extremity, and shook hands.

Let us look at literature. Foremost among the men of his day stands Pope, a man endowed with keen susceptibility, and with a wonderfully good ear for verse-music. He was wonderfully skilled, also, in the use of language, and it would be true to call him a French epigrameatist writing in English. Judged by the eye of the literary critic, Pope was as if made of the best-tempered wax ; the faintest force from the outside produced a clear impression. Pope's literary work, roughly speaking, falls into three divisions. Firstly, we have the Essay on Man, a smooth poetical version of the religion of the age ; secondly, the translation of Homer, exhibiting what was deemed the excellence of Augustan poetry ; and lastly, the Satires, which present faithfully the social characteristics, good, bad, and indifferent, which surrounded the poet.

To understand the Essay ·· Man must trace the lines of previous thought, and begin with Descartes (1596·1650). Descartes was painfully conscious of the imperfection of the *a priori* method; worked as it had been. He determined to build up a philosophy, and, feeling that he must have some undoubted starting point, he boldly turned on himself and exclaimed that *consciousness was the one sure thing*. This was no discovery ; it seemed like the reiteration of a part of a system which Descartes disliked. People had been aware of the importance of consciousness before the day of Descartes, but, with Descartes, consciousness was only the first link of a long chain, forged and put together by sheer thought, which aimed to be logical, if nothing else. So Descartes wrote his Discours de la Méthode, and, as may be inferred from the significant title, a new method was expounded. Moving from his aphoristic *cogito, ergo sum,* Descartes proclaimed that consciousness was the only ground of absolute certainty.

> " Know thyself, presume not God to scan ;
> The proper study of mankind is Man—"

sings Pope in the Second Epistle of the Essay, and again, at the conclusion of the poem, he proclaims :

> " And all our knowledge is OURSELVES TO KNOW."

We have not advanced beyond the Greek *know thyself,* but there is a quiet confidence in the trustworthiness of the introspective method which gives tone to Pope's moralizing and to much thought in his time. Although I am speaking more especially of Descartes just now, it may be well to mark the scornful way in which Pope disposes of the result of observation and experiment—Science :

> Go, wondrous creature ! mount where Science guides,
> Go, measure earth, weigh air, and state the tides ;
> Instruct the planets in what orbs to run,
> Correct old Time, and regulate the Sun ;
> Go, soar with Plato to th' empyreal sphere,
> To the first good, first perfect, and first fair ;
> Or tread the mazy round his follow'rs trod,
> And quitting sense call imitating God ;
> As Eastern priests in giddy circles run
> And turn their heads to imitate the Sun.
> *Go, teach eternal wisdom how to rule—*
> *Then drop into thyself, and be a fool !*

Descartes, to whom we return, interrogated his consciousness, and what clear replies he was able to educe, he maintained to be true. To put the matter in other and equivalent phrase, " what is clearly conceived is true." These are a few of the means by which Descartes proceeded to construct his system. 1. Never to accept anything as true but what is *evidently* so : to admit nothing but what so clearly presents itself as true that there can be no reason to doubt it. 2. To divide every question into as many separate questions as possible : that each fact being more easily conceived, the whole may be more intelligible. (Analysis). 3. To conduct the examination with order, beginning by that of objects the most simple, and therefore the easiest to be known, and ascending little by little up to knowledge the most complex. (Synthesis). 4. To make such exact calculations and circumspections as to be confident that nothing has been omitted. This, taken from G. H. Lewes's account of Descartes in his History of Philosophy, is what is called " the Deductive Method completely constructed."

When Descartes talked of the physical world—I need hardly remind you he was a great mathematician—he proclaimed the objective method to be the only guide : when he stepped from the path of scientific inquiry, he proclaimed the only guide to be the subjective method. He proceeded from causes to effects. Wise philosophy uses both methods, each in its own sphere : first, the objective to establish principles ; then, the principles *subjectively*, or rather *deductively*, to reason to particular instances which may happen to be presented for explanation.

Perhaps the chief object of Descartes' system was to prove the existence of God. On questioning his consciousness he found that he was finite, imperfect. But finite, imperfect, are co relative terms ; they imply infinite, perfect—that is, they imply God, the infinite, perfect being. My consciousness tells me this, and therefore I can no more doubt God's existence than I can my own. It is noteworthy that all this subjective formulating betrays a mathematical bent ; it was almost, nay, was, diagrammatic. Given consciousness as a mathematician is given a triangle, what can be deduced therefrom ?

From God, Descartes proceeded to discuss Body and Soul. *The essence of Body, of Substance, is that it occupies space, is extended.* One can suppose all attributes of matter as colour and weight taken away, but the occupancy of space, that is Extension, remains. *The essence of Mind is Thought.* Now, Thought and Extension are of different natures, and wholly exclusive ; therefore, Mind and Body are, in their fundamentals, distinct. It is also to be remembered that the doctrine of Innate Ideas, of ideas not dependent upon, or derived from, experience, are a necessary feature in the system of Descartes.

The method of Descartes was taken up and worked out to its logical conclusion by Spinoza. I quote G. H. Lewes : "Finally we may point to Spinozism as the legitimate result of that Subjective method which Descartes, in spite of his insurgence against Scholasticism, had restored to its ancient place. In vain were metaphysical entities and metaphysical theories banished ; their parent, the metaphysical method, was retained. That process of deduction which, as in Mathematics, from a few axioms constructed a whole universe, could only have been legitimised by an initial verification of the principles and a successive verification of the conclusions. This was not attempted, and could not have been effected, since the premises and the conclusions embrace objects inaccessible to human powers."

Then arose Thomas Hobbes, (1588-1679), the Sensationalist, who died only nine years before Pope was born. Hobbes maintained that the "original" of all thoughts "is that which we call *Sense*, for there is no conception in a man's mind which hath not at first, totally or by parts, been begotten upon the organs of Sense. The rest are derived from that original." Hobbes, then, is manifestly an opponent of Descartes, and he is also the forerunner of the French sensational school of the eighteenth century.

Then arose John Locke, (1632-1704), a typical Englishman, with a keen eye for observing and with a mind strongly analytical. He affirmed that there were *two* sources of Ideas, namely, Sensation (*objective*), and Reflection (*subjective*), the latter of which, by compounding the ideas already obtained by the former, created new ideas. Locke's general tone is similar to that of Hobbes.

Then arose Leibnitz, (1646-1714), with a Scholastic bent. He endeavoured to reconcile Science with Theology: He used the *a priori* method, as a matter of course, and contended that the essence of substance was force ; that a number of these forces or souls existed, *monads*, or metaphysical points ; that the natures of Mind and Body were not exclusive ; that a relation existed between the two which was sustained by " Pre-established Harmony "—they were as two clocks, each showing the same time, and each beating in unison with the other.

Then arose George Berkeley, (1684-1753), who swept away the duality of Mind and Body by becoming a pure Idealist and holding that all is Mind. To him stand opposed in terms, the Materialists, who sweep away the same duality and affirm that all is Matter.

The philosopher who had the greatest influence on Pope was Liebnitz. Pope was a mathematical philosopher ; very nice, finished, pointed, self-satisfied. There are are very few references to the Bible as an authority in the highest matters in the whole of his writings. This is to be expected, for Descartes and Spinoza looked upon truth as hidden in themselves, not as handed down from the remote past in forms which seemed unsatisfactory, and Liebnitz, although a "strayed Scholastic," was influenced greatly by the other two. It is not with the Essay on Man as with the Paradise Lost. In the Paradise Lost we have the creed and the symbolism of a highly concrete theology. So again, to look further back, the Essay on Man differs from the Faerie Queene. The Faerie Queene is full of philosophy, is grounded on philosophy : but then, that philosophy is derived from the Greeks and the Schoolmen. Pope held that his age was not the age of long moral epics, and would not write one. The men with whom Pope talked, among whom he moved, were enamoured of point and methodical treatment if only the conclusions to which they were led, did not conflict with their comfortable indifference. Sensitive and acute Pope reflects all this in his writings.

Lastly, Pope's day shows the genesis of Deism in England. The right to apply reason to Scripture is of French source. Faint murmers came before the thunder. Jeremy Taylor's Liberty of Prophesying is an argument for toleration just as much as John Locke's famous Essay in after-time. Chillingworth, Tillotson and Hobbes thought similarly to Jeremy Taylor and John Locke. Proceeding to Pope's period, we find that of the Deists the more remarkable are Bernard Mandeville, author of the Fable of the Bees ; Shaftesbury, Bolingbroke, John Toland, Matthew Tindal. Pope, plastic Pope, has the Deist mark, plain and unmistakable. His theology is the theology of logic—a pretty framework of something, but lacking the substance with which the framework is generally enveloped. Samuel Clarke's Sermons are in the same spirit ; they abound in axioms and deductions. Pope reasons, and places God afar off : a being to be contemplated, not one who has lively sympathy with man. All this was the outcome of much that was deemed unlovely and severe in orthodoxy. Pope could not paint Hell as Milton did; Hell is a subject of thought about which the set of men who influenced Pope gave themselves little thought. Critics who blame Pope for the omission do not see that, if he had followed their desires, he would have run counter to the spirit of his surroundings. To what conclusion, then, does Pope's logic lead him ? *Whatever is, is right.*

If Pope had been a thorough pantheist or a profound sceptic, he might have written a more powerful Poem, but it would not have been the polished Essay on Man, and it would have been at variance with a great deal of current thought. Pope said Homer was "correct." There was something "neat" in the old Classics, which critics like Addison could fall down and worship. As of the Classics, so of the Philosophy. It was "correct" and "neat" also, and not seldom in error. It banished superstition—we might add, enthusiasm ; it was cold, monotonous, and desperately gloomy in reaction. But even Edward Young's Night Thoughts have much in common with the point we have been discussing. Young meant to supplement Pope.

"Man, too, he *(Pope)* sung ; immortal man I sing."

Young is no seer who beholds visions and dreams dreams. He converts his infidel, as Pope might have done, by antithesis, epigram, and logic.

The Deists of the eighteenth century, although they were as thick as a swarm, suddenly vanished. Our business is not with these, but it ought to be mentioned here that their opponents often had no very fixed principles themselves. We can scarcely believe that Swift's theological beliefs were ardent. He detests Deists, not because he has founded his convictions upon inquiry, but because he said that to encourage heterodoxy was to overturn the established order of things, by which he was a gainer. What was established by law was right, and though Swift defends the Church in set terms in sermon and pamphlet, it would be going too far to assert that his defence means implicit faith in the Thirty-nine Articles. Other men there were who, no doubt, disliked Deism heartily. Robinson Crusoe (Defoe's character is not easy to fathom) is a vehement protester against Deism. Samuel Richardson, the novelist, felt a strong compunction against introducing anything savouring of indfielity. Samuel Johnson, a thoroughly good but bigoted soul, had a deep-seated contempt for unbelievers in sacred matters. One might add to the roll, and then proceed to talk about the powerful reaction against the negativeness of Pope's day, which produced a Wesley and a Whitfield, but it would be to defeat the object of this brief paper.

C. E. M.

COLLEY CIBBER.

It is difficult at this distance of time to form a correct idea of the character of a man so little remembered as Colley Cibber. He seems to have been of quick wit and superficial talents, but his genius was not sufficient to make any lasting impression upon time ; a star perhaps, but one that shed an uncertain light and was soon eclipsed. He was highly esteemed as a dramatist during his day, and we must not overlook the merit he had, because Pope's spiteful mind abused him in his Dunciad. Indeed, Pope finding that it was necessary to have a prince of dunces, seems to have chosen Cibber not so much from his fitness for the quasi honour, as from lack of a man more suitable. His genius lay in dramatic power. Pope systematically professed to sneer at the drama ; and indeed a man who seems to have recognized neither virtue nor power in Shakespeare was hardly fit to find the comparatively scattered grains of talent among the chaff of Cibber's mind. But let us look a little more carefully into the details of his life and his mode of living.

Colley Cibber was born in London on the 6th of November, 1671, in Southampton street, facing Southampton House. His father, Caius Gabriel Cibber, was a native of Holstein, who had come to England some time before the restoration of Charles II., to follow his profession which was that of statuary. The basso-relievo on the pedestal of the great column in London and the two figures of the lunatics (the raving and the melancholy) over the gates of Bethlehem Hospital, are no ill monuments of his fame as an artist. His mother was the daughter of a William Colley who belonged to the ancient family of Glaiston in Rutlandshire. The child was called Colley to preserve the family name which otherwise would have become extinct, his mother being the only surviving representative. When ten years of age, the boy was sent to a free school in Lincolnshire. He passed through the complete course given there, but had no further collegiate training, and, as he himself says, never improved his store of learning by after reading or study. He speaks of himself when at school, as " always in full spirits, in some small capacity to do right, but in a more frequent alacrity to do wrong, and consequently often under a worse character than he wholly deserved." A giddy negligence seems to have always possessed him, and even in later life this appears to have directed much of his conduct. He was very free from jealousy but could not resist holding up others, even his friends, to ridicule. The child was father of the man. Even at school we find one of his friends turning against him, because the lad said, " You are always jeering and making a jest of me to every boy in the school." Cibber confesses that he brought " many a mischief" upon himself by the same folly in riper life. He had not sense enough to know that he hurt the feelings of others by his witty remarks, and they in return hated him because they had not sense enough to know that he did not intend to hurt them. One of his strongest characteristics seems to have been personal pride—a pride so great that he gloried not only in his virtues but even in his follies and openly avowed them. It was this that enabled him almost to take pleasure in Pope's Satires against him. Pope of course ridiculed Cibber's weak points ; but in so doing he seems not to have known that in reality he was pleasing Cibber, for so great was his vanity and egotism that he would rather be known to posterity by his follies and want of genius, than not be known at all. He almost takes it as a compliment to be made the central figure, if even among dunces, for he says : "Pope must consider that my face and name are more known than those of many thousands of more consequence in the kingdom, and that therefore I will be a sure bait to catch him readers." This pride seldom could be wounded, for anything said against him he considered either false or said through envy or stupidity.

But to return to his life. At the age of sixteen having been refused admittance to Winchester College he enlisted under the Earl of Devonshire in support of William of Orange, but he did not find a soldier's life congenial. Even this bloodless campaign frightened him from the field ; for we have every reason to believe that it was sheer timidity that prevented his regular enlistment. He returned to London, but there found little regular employment. It was at this period that he appears to have first seriously thought of becoming an actor, and it is certain that his want of work led him to become a constant attendant at the theatres. At the age of eighteen, he was first engaged to act a minor part, but was in receipt of no salary for some nine months. A curious tale is told of the manner of his first becoming a hired actor. While on the stage one night he became so terrified as to forget his part, causing an awkward hitch in the play. Betterton, the chief actor, asked in some anger, who the young fellow was who had committed the blunder. He was told, "Master Colley." 'Then forfeit him his wages" replied Betterton. "Why sir," said the other, "he has no salary." "Then," said the old man, "put him down ten shillings a-week and forfeit him five."

His choice of a theatrical life was in direct opposition to his parents' wishes, for the profession was then most justly considered one of the lowest ; but he recognised his own qualifications for the position : and to do him justice we must own that he did his best during his public life to reform the more flagrant abuses connected with the stage. As an actor, his success in the end was great. A weak voice was against him, but the principle hindrance in his career was inability to work smoothly with his fellow actors. He was indeed so unpopular, that, some four years later, we find him in receipt of only twenty shillings per week Notwithstanding his poverty, in 1693 he ventured on matrimony, and in order the better to eke out his livelihood he begun to write for the stage. Still he won his way but slowly. By the recommendation of Congreve he had the honour of acting a principal part in The Double Dealer, played before Queen

Mary. Mr. Congreve was pleased with his performance, and even spoke to the managers, asking them to employ Cibber regularly. But they preferred their own actors ; and we do not find him again taking any prominent part for some time. The production of a prologue which was accepted and spoken by him, brought him into considerable notice, and he was allowed to take part in the next play. This afforded him an opportunity to astonish his fellow performers. The expediency of writing a part suitable for his own acting, led to his compos- ing the comedy of Love's Last Shift. This was produced in 1695, and his success in portraying the character of Sir Novelty, placed him upon a footing with the first actors of the day. His next play The Non-Juror was his most popular production, owing probably to its political character ; and for it receiv- ed the then very unusual price of one hundred guineas. This play was levelled against the Jacobite party and seems to have afforded the principal reason for Cibber's being made Poet Laureate. Great discontent was expressed that the laurel of the nation should be conferred upon a comedian ; and some idea of Cibber's provoking humour may be formed from a fact in connection with this appointment. On this occasion, "the public papers were enlivened with in- genious epigrams and satirical flirts." The witty author, caring little for what was said against him, in comparison to the pleasure of doing something peculiar, entered the lists and published a set of doggerel verses in which he lampoon- ed himself. Ten years after the successful appearance of The Non-Juror, Cib- ber produced his last and best play,—The Careless Husband. Its popularity may be judged of from the fact that it was acted for twenty-eight nights to- gether, and that the total receipts were found to be one hundred and forty pounds. This was an amount that had not been equalled by any play, during the previous fifty years.

But Cibber's health was failing. Several, of his old fellow-workers too, were obliged from various causes to leave their favourite stage and green-room at nearly the same time, and Cibber felt that he too must leave all active work to others. He is described at this time as being "in tolerably good taste," but "that he went about ever gold-laced, highly powdered, scented and diamoned, and dispensing graceful bows ; bestowing praises on whoever had the good luck to be dead, and satire on all who were here to enjoy it." During the remainder of his days he amused himself by writing his Apology for the Life of Mr. Colley Cibber, an entertaining work which is in itself sufficient to disprove the charge brought against him by Pope, of being the chief of dunces.

E. D.

EDWARD YOUNG, 1684-1785.

Edward Young was born at Upham, a village near Winchester, in 1684. His father was for many years Rector of Upham and a Royal Chaplain. He was afterwards made Dean of Salisbury, and died in that town in 1705, when his son had just completed his twenty-first year.

Young was educated at Winchester School and at All Souls' College, Oxford. Tindal, who was a frequent visitor at Oxford, says of him :—"All the other boys I can always answer, because I know whence they have their arguments, which I have read a hundred times, but that fellow Young is always pestering me with something of his own." When about twenty-six he began to write poems, some of which were printed in the Tatler. A few years later he wrote several odes and poems, which he addressed to persons in authority. Of these The Last Day is the most remarkable. It consists of a description of the end of the world, as Young would have it arranged; but the field here provided for his imagination is too large. He loses himself among the wonders and horrors of his own creation, and spoils the poem by his extravagance of violence.

In 1714 he took the degree of B. C. L., and at this time he must have had a considerable reputation, for he was appointed at the foundation of the Codrington Library to deliver the Latin oration. He was then tutor to Lord Burleigh, son of the Earl of Exeter, but in 1719 he left his service for that of the Duke of Wharton, whose favour he thought worth cultivating.

We notice in his youth, and all through his life, a constant striving for social position, and an earnest perseverance in the matter which was worthy of a nobler aim : his efforts in this direction were crowned with but small success, though the time allotted him for his operations was unusually long. We must admire, at least, the durability of a conviction which, at the close of an unsuccessful campaign of eighty years, is still as firm and potent as at the outset.

The Duke of Wharton persuaded Young to come forward as a political candidate, providing him with means to defray the necessary expenses, but this was an unsuccessful attempt—Young was defeated, and emerged from the fray considerably richer in experience, but not otherwise benefited. The expenses of the election, also, were found to be largely in excess of the means provided by the Duke, so that pecuniary difficulties were added to the candidate's other troubles.

He continued, however, to write industriously both prose and poetry, taking care always to address his works to one or other of those who sit in high places, and thus, through occasional successes, made his livelihood.

Out of this literary and political turmoil we are surprised, in 1727, to find Mr. Young steering his bark into the calm haven of the church.

He took orders at the age of forty-three and was appointed a Royal Chaplain. Two years later he was presented by the College of All Souls with the Rectory of Welwyn, in Hertfordshire.

In this "humble shade"—his "heart at rest"—Young passed thirty-five years of his life, the beauties of nature with which he was surrounded providing him a rich garner whence to supply his busy brain.

He was accustomed to resort for daily exercise to the churchyard, where he walked and meditated among the graves of departed parishioners. We think his choice of a promenade ground is open to discussion, but as we are further told that he was naturally of a lively and genial disposition, it is to be supposed that he adopted this habit in order to preserve the balance of power and to prevent hilarity getting the better of him.

In 1731 Young took a bold stride into the ranks of aristocracy, and chose therefrom a wife—a lady both in name and nature.

She was the daughter of the Earl of Lichfield and widow of Colonel Lee, and with her Young spent ten years of happy married life. Her two children found in him the affection of a father and in the Rectory at Welwyn all the joys of home.

Young at this time wrote some odes, and letters to Voltaire and Pope, none of which were of much merit.

In 1736 one of Lady Young's daughters, who had married a son of Lord Palmerston, died at Nice, whither she had gone for her health, accompanied by her husband and parents. Seven months later her sister was cut off, and in 1741 Lady Elizabeth Young herself died—a crowning sorrow for Young, who was now left alone with his son, a child of seven years.

It was these sad misfortunes which prompted Young—still in the prime of life—to compose his Night Thoughts, the work by which he is best known, and which, with two or three of his other writings, will always take high rank in English Literature.

Taine, with what we think unjust severity, describes Young as "a clergyman and courtier, who, having vainly attempted to enter Parliament, then to become a Bishop, married, lost his wife and children, and made use of his misfortunes to write meditations on Life, Death, Immortality," etc., etc. That his grief for the loss of a virtuous wife was sincere we cannot doubt, and the sad circumstances which attended the death and burial of his daughters in a foreign land were calculated to stir into voice a far less poetic soul than Young's.

The principal beauty of the Night Thoughts is found in the metaphors and imagery with which it abounds, and quite apart from its merits as a poem, the good service it has done the cause of religion is a point in its favour which should not be forgotten.

The Night Thoughts were published from 1742 to 1746. Between this date and his death Young wrote several Satires and a Letter on Original Composition, addressed to Richardson the Novelist, which is fresh and full of vigour, though the writer was then in his seventy-fifth year. One of Young's tragedies, The Revenge, is still sometimes produced on the stage. His Odes were signal failures, but the Love of Fame, a series of Satires, brought out his peculiar talents, and met with well-deserved favour.

Young died at Welwyn at the advanced age of eighty-one. We read of him working in his garden and entertaining his visitors with lively conversation when he was too old for public work. Four years before his death he was made Clerk of the Closet to the Princess Dowager of Wales. This was no small gratification to him—though late, yet far better than never. This, with the Royal Chaplaincy, was, notwithstanding all his pains, the only preferment he ever reached.

In conclusion, we may say Young's influence, both on his own time and by his writings, was a good one. We have to remember that he lived in an age of flattery and insincerity, and his failings were less blameworthy than those of many of his contemporaries. In private life he was above suspicion, and it may be supposed that the devotion of the latter half of his life atoned for the wild oats we are told he sowed in his youth.

I: T. G.

LETTER–WRITING DURING THE EIGHTEENTH CENTURY.

I have been asked to make some remarks on the subject of letter-writing, and to give examples of the different styles of epistolary communication among the writers of the Eighteenth, and the beginning of the Nineteenth, century.

The letters of such celebrated English writers as Pope, Addison, Lord Chesterfield, Horace Walpole, Lady Mary Wortley Montague; also the French and German, and perhaps better-known, writings of Mme. de Sévigné, Mme. de Stael, Voltaire, Goethe, and others, combine not only questions of politics, religion, and science, but also deal with the more commonplace (!) subjects of love and friendship.

Pope's letters are admirable specimens of prose composition—full of humour, wit, and vivacity, but too studiously elaborate to be models of epistolary style. His Abelard and Eloisa, though fine as a poem, is finer as a piece of high-wrought eloquence. No woman could be supposed to write a better love-letter in verse.

Addison is distinguished from almost all the great masters of ridicule by the grace, nobleness, and moral purity, which we find, even in his merriment. His mirth is always consistent, with tender compassion for all that is frail, and with profound reverence for all that is sublime. His merits as an author need no other testimony than the emphatic summary of Johnson—"As a describer of life and manners he must be allowed to stand, perhaps the first of the first rank. As a teacher of wisdom, he may be confidently followed. All the enchantment of fancy, and all the cogency of argument are employed to recommend to the reader his real interest, the care of pleasing the Author of his being. Whoever wishes to attain an English style, familiar but not coarse, and elegant but not ostentatious, must give his days and nights to the volumes of Addison."

Of Lord Chesterfield's letters, Lord Macaulay says, that he stands much lower in the estimation of posterity than if they had never been published—but men ought to be judged by the places in which they live, and the state of society by which they are surrounded. I do not wish to defend Chesterfield's faults, but must speak of his virtues. Not one father in those days was so good, so tender and so wise. He tells his son that he always frequented the company of his superiors, and his superiors he reckoned not only by their rank. "Dr. Swift and Mr. Pope," he says, "condescended to admit me into their company, and though they had no titles and I was an Earl, I always felt that I was obliged by their politeness, and was favoured by being allowed to converse with them."

Are there many noblemen who would say so now-a-days? No, not many Popes, Swifts—nor, l·t us add, Chesterfields.

Of Horace Walpole's letters there is scarcely any writer in whose work it would be possible to find so many contradictory judgments, so many sentences of extravagant nonsense. Nor was it only in his familiar correspondence that he wrote in this flighty and inconsistent manner, but in long and elaborate books; in books repeatedly transcribed and intended for the public eye. He sneered at everybody and put the worst construction on every action—

> " Turned every man the wrong side out,
> And never gave to truth and virtue that
> Which simpleness and merit purchaseth."

If we adopt the classification which Akenside has given of the pleasures of imagination, we should say that with the sublime and beautiful, Walpole had nothing to do, but that the third province, the odd, was his peculiar domain. His letters, on the whole, are perhaps the most entertaining in the language, and the productions by which he will be best known. His style is singularly easy and appropriate, and the superabundance of scandal, gossip, wit, epigram, and anecdote gives to every page a special attraction. In spite of his want of accuracy and veracity, which, according to Hallam, renders his testimony comparatively worthless, his correspondence and memoirs will always hold a conspicuous place in literature, from the fact that the author had learned the art of writing what people will like to read.

Lady Mary Wortley Montague's letters display great intelligence, wisdom, careful observation, and a raciness, sprightliness, and elegance of style of which there are still few examples. Those written while abroad and descriptive of the court and society of Vienna, of the scenery and customs of the East, of the antiquities, baths, mosques, etc., are among the finest in literature. At Belgrade Lady Mary first observed the practice of inoculation for small-pox, and her letters on that subject excited much attention among medical men, and were instrumental in introducing inoculation into England.

In Mme. de Sévigné's letters to her daughter, we have the most beautiful illustrations of maternal affection, and of true friendship. She does not come under the "we" of Shakespeare: "Who are creatures that look before and after; the more surprising that we do not look round a little at what is passing under our very eyes," for no occurrence in every-day life was too trifling to be commented upon. The charm of her style is so great, and her descriptions so powerful and natural, that her readers are carried away, and in fancy mingle with her in the society of the time, of which her letters give such a true and detailed account.

As for the character of Voltaire, it will be, as it long has been, variously judged. His literary merits admit of less doubt, and posterity has confirmed the sentiment of his contemporaries, that he was the sovereign writer of his country. He was its author-king. No other writer controlled so completely the opinions of the world. Yet he was not a great thinker, not a great poets not a great historian, and not a great novelist. If we seek for the secret of his success, we must turn to those lighter compositions, stories, tales, vers de societé, madrigals, letters, and epigrams, in which the spirit of the age saw itself expressed with inimitable vivacity, grace, point, and agreeableness. He was there the master of all styles, save in his own phrase, of the ennuyeux, or dull and wearisome.

To give further examples of other equally noted writers of this period would I fear, gain me, if I have not already merited, Voltaire's criticism of himself, so I will conclude by making a few remarks on letter-writing generally. Good letter-writing is one of the strongest connecting links of life, and, as such deserves to take a high rank in the literature of all ages. Who does not know the delight of communication with distant friends! The comfort of writing off a load of worries where you are sure of sympathy! Then, too, consider the satisfaction of gratified vanity in the development of new ideas, which, until written, you did not know you possessed. In newspaper correspondence, for example, what a field for imagination run riot!

In considering business letters, brevity, literally, is the soul of wit, while as for a love-letter, most people would be inclined to agree, that brevity need not be a chief characteristic.

"Que les lettres des amis absents sont délicieuses à recevoir! Si les portraits des amis séparés par la distance ravivent leur mémoire et trompent le regret par une vaine et decevante consolation, combien plus ces lettres qui sont eux-mêmes, qui portent les véritables empreintes de l'ami absent!.... Grâce soit rendue à Dieu de ce qu'au moins la haine ne nous défend pas d'être ainsi l'un à l'autre presents."

E. B.

SHAKESPEARE AND HIS PLAY
RICHARD II.

———

The curiosity, which, inherent in the human race, finds a legitimate sphere in the domain of letters, has ever been roused by the name of Shakespeare. For over two centuries and a-half, mankind has possessed an unrivalled collection of dramatic works, and if it were not for a church register, we should be as ignorant of their reputed author, as we are of Homer. That William Shakespeare was born in humble circumstances, in a remote part of England during 1564; that he married Anne Hathaway, and had three children; that he died in 1616, and was buried in his native place, are almost the only facts connected with his personal history. Nothing of any moment remains to illustrate what must have been his extraordinary life in London, and even after the production of his works, ''he abandoned them with perfect indifference, to oblivion or to fame." Indeed, according to Holmes, "no original manuscript of any play or poem, letter or other prose composition in the handwriting of Shakespeare, has ever been discovered, none is known to have been preserved, within the reach of the remotest definite tradition."

It is not a matter for wonder, therefore, that so soon as the wave of Puritan fanaticism had subsided, and the taste for French plays which came in with the restoration, had been lost, that the labours and the history of this marvellous man, gradually attracted the attention of the learned. The curiosity then awakened, has steadily increased; Germany and America have equalled England, in their homage to his genius, till the world has claimed him as a citizen, and enrolled him among those she will not willingly let die.

The age of Shakespeare is a memorable one in the annals of English History; but it is not to be believed, that the great men of the day were formed upon the moment; rather is it necessary to go back some fifty years, to what we should almost be inclined to consider the most memorable epoch. The rise of the New Learning filled England with a newer life, and prepared the way for the reception of the Reformation, with its ennobling doctrines, which quickened the energies, and produced a deeper sympathy with all that was great or good or beautiful. Shakespeare lived when the Reformation had been accomplished; he adorned and filled with undying fame the end of a period of advancement, and though "he possessed no Greek nor Latin store," yet the very air he breathed was so full of wonders, so brightened with the dawn of a new philosophy which he strongly felt, that the power of his genius enabled him to assimilate everything to his own use. It was then that Bacon, Spenser, and Shakespeare with others who were creative genuises, collected the wisdom of the past, and either cast it totally aside, or purified it in the crucible of their minds; it was then that the world received that mighty impulse which loosened thought, and started her upon a period of intellectual prosperity, which has lasted until our day; and the messages these men delivered, are waiting now, amid the vast increase of learning, to be taken up by a master-mind and re arranged with the whole, in the glorious march of progress.

In order, however, to understand Shakespeare's work, let us briefly glance at the state of the drama. Before his time, we are told, "the mysteries and miracle plays, in which Adam and Eve appeared almost nude, and in which Noah's wife boxed the ears of the patriarch before entering the ark, had fallen into disuse;" so also had the "moralities," and the pageants and masks in honour of royalty, and it was not till after the Reformation that a change for the better begin, when the Inns of the Court and the Universities vied with each other in the production of plays." The theatre, Green says, "was commonly the court-yard of an inn, with a few covered seats for the wealthier spectators, a few flowers served to indicate a garden, and armies were represented by a dozen scene-shifters, with swords and bucklers; heroes rode in and out on hobby-horses, and a scroll on a post told whether the plot was at Athens or London." But before the close of Elizabeth's reign, and when Shakespeare was in his prime, all this had disappeared. Eighteen theatres existed in London and "the intellectual quickening of the age had reached the mass of the people." The use of blank verse in tragedy had been introduced, and the success of the new drama assured. Here we see vividly the gradual growth to a state of perfection, and one is enabled to understand more clearly the vast power of that mind, which, in absorbing all that was good, fearlessly cast aside the trammels of a classical model, great as its use had been, and out of a mixture of "bombast, dullness and buffonery," created the British stage.

It would be mere pedantry on my part, to attempt to relate the cause of Shakespeare's flight from Stratford-upon-Avon, and his arrival in London about 1588, or to say anything of his friendship with the "romantic Earl of Southampton," or to draw your attention towards any of his dramas, save Richard II., which appears to have been among the first of his productions, and which can be traced in print to 1597. It may not, however, be out of place, to take a brief retrospect of the history of the ti ne, ere we can rightly comprehend this—the most admirable of all the historical plays. The England of the period, was in a state of ferment, not unlike the Ireland of to-day. Richard, to quote Green, "had alienated every class of his subjects. He had estranged the nobles by his peace policy, the landowners by his refusal to sanction the insane measures of repression they directed against the labourer, the merchant-class by his illegal exactions, and the Church by his shelter of the Lollards." Through all this, however, he might have stool alone, for the "divinity which doth hedge a king" was fully acknowledged, had not the act of "jealousy and tyranny from fear of the House of Lancaster," with which the play opens, "roused up an unscrupulous leader." The banishment of Bolingbroke, "was soon succeeded by his outlawry; and on his father's death, he found himself deprived of his titles and estates. At this moment, Richard had crossed into Ireland, to complete the work of conquest, and Bolingbroke, urged by the Arch-Bishop of Arundel, an exile like himself, eluded the vigilance of the French Court, and landed on the Coast of Yorkshire." The sequel is known to all; as we follow Shakespeare, we see "a vivid and faithful picture of the reign of Richard, his character being drawn with a fidelity and beauty of execution, which renders it invaluable as a mere historical portrait. The other characters are also faithful embodiments, while the real incidents of Richard's eventful life, for which it is said Shakespeare was indebted to Holinshed, are pourtrayed with such perfect truth, that the whole play forms a glowing picture of the most romantic and picturesque period of English History." The action of the piece commences early in 1398, and ends toward the latter part of 1400. The sketch of John of Gaunt proves interesting to us, when we remember, that it was with him that Wyclif "allied himself in the first effort he made for the Reform of the Church." So great an influence did the theatre now exert over the minds of the English people, that the scene in Act IV., relating to the deposition of Richard, was omitted on the first appearance, for fear of offending Elizabeth. Subsequently, the leaders in the rebellion of Essex, a short time before their outbreak, produced the entire play in order to prepare the nation for revolution. Indeed, as we have already remarked, so powerful was the divinity of kings, that we can well admire the fearlessness of the Poet in placing in the mouth of Richard that well-known soliloquy of Act III., Scene II., where the distracted monarch, labouring under despondency, proposes "with rainy eyes, To write sorrow on the bosom of the Earth * * * to sit upon the ground, And tell sad stories of the death of kings." Never had English ears heard a king moan like that, and when further on, we read, that he bids his courtiers cover their heads "and mock not flesh and blood With solemn reverence," for he lives on bread like them, feels want, and needs the sympathy of friends, it is not difficult to understand the effect the play must have had upon the people ; it was a lesson in democracy, a glimpse behind the mask, and answered to our modern nitroglycerine. Shakespeare's love of country seems to have been a marked characteristic ; we meet it continually, but no where so strongly as in the historical dramas. It has been mainly instrumental in popularizing them with the great mass of Englishmen. Sprung from the people, he knew their inner thoughts, "their love of hard fighting, their faith in the doom that waits upon triumphant evil, their pity for the fallen," and the farewell of Bolingbroke to his country, must have been no hap-hazard sentence, for the glory of the triumph over the Armada, was doubtless ringing in his ears—

> " Then, England's ground, farewell ; sweet soil, adieu ;
> My mother, and my nurse, that bears me yet !
> Where'er I wander, boast of this I can,
> Though banished, yet a true-born Englishmen."

There are yet two points in his character which remain to be noticed, for they appear prominently in Richard II. The first is, his love of music ; the seconds his wonderful imagination :

Music, in its truest sense, that is to say, the music of the master-minds of Germany, appeals to man as the language of another world. As Herbert Spencer remarks, "it unfolds the sympathetic side of our nature, and yields an indefinite impression of an unknown ideal life, and its intenser delights.' Under its influence we feel ennobled, all our better feelings are drawn out, 'til we rise up refreshed and invigorated ; we have been in contact with harmony' have heard sounds that are immortal, sounds that are not new, which come upon the spirit, as if in recollections from afar, and as our earthy natures for the moment disappear, we float out upon "the tides of a golden sea, setting towards Eternity."

In Act II., Scene I., Shakespeare writes, that "the tongues of dying men enforce attention like deep harmony." What greater tribute has been paid music than this ? The last utterances of man, when truth becomes sublime, likened to the just adaptation of parts to each other, which is harmony : and to have this, is to have truth. Music is, therefore, truth, and accordingly, as the Poet writes, in another place, "The man that hath no music in himself, Nor is not moved with concord of sweet sounds, Is fit for treasons, stratagems and spoils."

The Imagination of Shakespeare, is visible on every page ; it is this faculty, predominating so much in him, which carries us along, and without the aid of representation, enables us to see as in a panorama, the scenes he is portraying. Especially is this the case in Act V., Scenes IV., and V., describing the death of Richard, which he brings before us with all the terror of stern reality. The power of Imagination is the chief point to be taken account of, in gauging the value of poetry, and the cultivation of this faculty, by the study of poetry, is one of the three things, for a polite education, insisted upon by Bacon, in his Advancement of Learning. In Addison's letters upon the Imagination, which we have read this year, he remarks, that English Poets in this respect are the greatest, but that Shakespeare "has incomparably excelled all others." He continues to add, "there is something so wild, and yet so solemn, in the speeches of Shakespeare's ghosts, fairies, witches, and the like imaginary persons, that we cannot forbear thinking them natural, though we have no rule by which to judge them, and must confess if there are such things in the world, it looks highly probable they should talk and act as he has represented them."

During the three years this Literary Society has existed, our attention has been mainly directed to Poetry, and it may not be out of place to ask, what is its end and aim ? In its truest form, poetry is the reflex of civilization ; it has ever accompanied the destinies of a nation, has refined its vigorous manhood, and cast a glory over its full maturity. It is not therefore to be monopolized as the food of love-sick maidens, and sentimental young men. This is its misfortune, and no doubt accounts for the expressions of scarce-concealed contempt we hear occasionally applied to it. On the other hand, to him who is capable of appreciation, the magic and the witchery of verse, convey a deep consolation ; they soothe the man of business, and drive away the cares of the statesman. Poetry elevates man, it drives him out of himself, and places him nearer to that ideal, which every one at some time or another has formed ; it gives him then an opportunity of taking a retrospect, and animated by its power, he will form anew his resolutions; it fills him, too, as we have said of music, with a refining influence, and who can say this is not a great good, operating beneficially on the excited life he is obliged to lead, in the eternal race for gold. But to be more ethical, and to quote Bacon, "the use of Poetry is to demonstrate and illustrate, that which is taught or delivered, as by a thousand moral paintings ;" and thus, poetry is a science; it systematizes all things, and becomes a medium through which we receive the impression of what is great, noble, and true ; and is in the language of Keats a friend

"To soothe the cares and lift the thoughts of man."

Although this may be the general aim of poetry, what is the particular teaching of Shakespeare ? Here it is, in the words of Judge Holmes : "To perceive and to know the virtues and crimes of men, to reflect them as in a mirror, and to exhibit them in their sources, their nature, their workings, and their results, and in such a way as to exclude chance, and to banish arbitrary fate, which can have no place in a well-ordered world—this is a task which Shakespeare has imposed upon the poet and himself."

The mind and soul of Shakespeare were full of genius, I mean genius apart from talent, which is a different thing, and, as Coleridge puts it, may be inherited, but the other, never ; his eyes must have sparkled with the heaven-born fire ; the world has seen but few like him, and they alone know how to please the thought-throned mind, or can attempt, as Kirke White sings—

```
    *    *    *    'from her fleshy seat to draw
To realms where Fancy's golden orbits roll,
Disdaining all but 'wildering Rapture's law,
    The captivated soul.
```

S. G. W. M.

ANONYMOUS LITERATURE.

There are in our language many words whose *sound* is more quickly expressive than is their *appearance* in type or handwriting; words which one loves, in reading, to utter alou l; wor ls that seem to have a flavonr for the palate, and a substance for the tongue, as well as music for the ear.

These are the words most easily recalled by the reader of verses, and, on that account, the words most commonly associated with the names of the gentler and the more exhilarating writers of song. Who is there who reads the *Lays of Ancient Rome* with unmoved tongue or lip ? Do we not seem to taste such words as these ?

> " Meanwhile the Tuscan army,
>   Right glorious to behold,
> Came flashing back the noonday light,
> Rank behind rank, like surges bright
>   On a broad sea of gold.
>
> " Four hundred trumpets sounded
>   A peal of warlike glee,
> As that great host with measured tread,
> And spears advaneed, and ensigns spread,
> Roll'd slowly toward the bridge's head
>   Where stood the dauntless three."

We have, on the other hand, many words fixed in our memory by *sight* rather than by sound—words one takes no pleasure in articulating—words which, sometimes, when come suddenly upon, shunt a train of thought on to a siding with a jar, and leave the disturbed reader with his bewildered head thrust out of a window, with a " where are we ?"

Anonymous

is such a word. Does it not, at first sight, fill one with a vague sense of inse-curity—like a suspicion of malaria ? Does it not drag before one's mind the names of such dishonest parents as Malevolence and Cowardice—and the long procession of its offspring—Blackmail, Ostracism, Terrrorism, and Nihilism, its youngest born ? Ugly as the word is, it has a long-standing companionship with literatnre—a melancholy one too often—and it is for this reason that I dare to night to recognize an acquaintance apparently so disreputable. A writer of to-day (Matthews) says :—" Even the homeliest and most familiar words, the most hackneyed phrases, are connected by imperceptible ties with the hopes and fears, the reasonings and reflections of bygone men and times." And Archbishop Trench remarks :—" Many a single word is itself a concentrated poem." Words, then, would seem to have a sort of personality, and some words, like some people, are to be judged from their surroundings ; I would like to-night to bespeak (a good word) for Anonymous by telling you where I have met him. While this inquiring circle has sat in judgment upon the irreproachable Addison, and has chaffed the warm-hearted Steele ; while we have chided ths sightless Milton, and kicked our brazen heels on the tomb at Stratford, the oldest and most prolific of authors has hitherto escaped our innocent criticism.

Yet here we have writers who have taken their undisputed seats, from time to time, amongst the most noble knights of the disordered table.

Have not Bacon, Chatterton, Byron, Scott and Dickens sat beside them— with an uneasy pleasure it may be—proud to share (and perhaps not too reluctant to appreciate) the smiles intended for their shadowy neighbours ?

If, while introducing *Anonymous* to you to-night, I have had to bring along his titled relative *Pseudonymous*, I beg that you will permit him to remain unchallenged amongst us. They have both put forth riddles, which learning has sometimes found hard to guess, and sometimes wholly unanswerable.

I do not wish to speak to you of *Junius*, whose once-dreaded name rises at the first mention of my theme—nor of Chatterton's celebrated impostures, sadly familiar to you all—nor yet of the greatest as well as the oldest of Anonymoua poems—*the Book of Job* —of which it has been said, " As a work both of genius and art it occupies well-nigh the first rank in Hebrew literature, and is unsurpassed in sublimity of imagination by any poem of antiquity."

Nor do I care to say much of the many noble derelicts—such as *Auld Robin Gray, Rejected Addresses, Waverley, Beautiful Snow, The Changed Cross*— which floated, unclaimed, upon the sea of publicity, until time proved them seaworthy.

It is not of these that I would speak, but of some of the humbler of the still vizored knights.

Turning back to childhood we remember who sang us to sleep in the rhymes of Mother Goose -- *Anonymous*. Who penned the thrilling tales in yellow covers, which at the age of fourteen, made Kingston seem tedious and Ballantyne commonplace ?--*Anonymous*. Yes, and who of us is there who treasures no favourite lines of this unknown friend, who has felt what we feel, and spoken as we wish we could ?

Touching stories have been told of the popularity of *Annie Laurie* a Scottish song, which every English person can repeat. Does not every one regret to call it *Anonymous?* There is another widely-known poem called the *Veni Creator* (Come Holy Ghost our souls inspire), whose author we would gladly call our friend. What a pleasant fellow must have been the writer of the *Vicar of Bray.* One can fancy the jovial hours flying in his company. Was the affecting ballad beginning

" There were three crows sat on a tree,"

an after-dinner impromptu, or did the talented author worry his wits about it as I have lately worried mine ? How many beautiful and quaint conceits are gathered within the covers of *Percy's Reliques* and Scott's *Minstrelsy of the Border.* Yes, and how many exquisite lines blossom and are lost in the ephemeral columns of the newspapers—lost, sometimes to be brought to light years afterwards, and sadly classified with the " found drowned " of literature— *Anonymous !*

I have had but time to skim over the surface of this dead sea, but I would like to suggest that we devote one evening before the close of the session, to the gathering of some of the beautiful crystals which a little searching would reveal. May it be permitted to close this *outline* sketch with the celebrated lines to a skeleton ?

F. T.

TO A SKELETON.

Behold this ruin ! 'twas a skull
Once of ethereal spirit full.
This narrow cell was Life's retreat,
This space was Thought's mysterious seat.
What beautous visions fill'd this spot !
What dreams of pleasure long forgot !
Nor hope, nor joy, nor love, nor fear,
Have left one trace of record here.

Beneath this mouldering canopy
Once shone the bright and busy eye,
But start not at the dismal void,—
If social love that eye employed ;
If with no lawless fire it gleam'd,
But through the dews of kindness beam'd,—
That eye shall be for ever bright
When stars and sun are sunk in night.

Within this hollow cavern hung
The ready, swift and tuneful tongue ;
If Falsehood's honey it disdained,
And when it could not praise was chain'd ;
If bold in Virtue's cause it spoke,
Yet gentle concord never broke,—
This silent tongue shall plead for thee
When Time unveils Eternity !

Say, did these fingers delve the mine ?
Or with the envied rubies shine ?
To hew the rock or wear the gem
Can little now avail to them.
But if the page of truth they sought,
Or comfort to the mourner brought,
These hands a richer meed shall claim
Then all that wait on wealth and fame.

Avails it whether bare or shod
These feet the paths of duty trod ?
If from the bowers of Ease they fled,
To seek Affliction's humble shed :
If Granleur's guilty bribe they spurned,
And home to Virtue's cot returned,—
These feet with Angel wings shall vie,
And tread the palace of the sky !

The MS. of this poem was found near a skeleton in the London Royal College of Surgeons, about 1820. The author has never been found, though a reward of fifty guineas was offered for his discovery.

www.ingramcontent.com/pod-product-compliance
Lightning Source LLC
Chambersburg PA
CBHW031321280626
47169CB00019B/2601